THE RECKONING

ALSO BY KRIS GREENE

The Dark Storm
The Demon Hunt

THE RECKONING

Kris Greene

ST. MARTIN'S GRIFFIN
NEW YORK

First published in the United States by St. Martin's Griffin,
an imprint of St. Martin's Publishing Group

THE RECKONING. Copyright © 2019 by Kris Greene.
All rights reserved. Printed in the United States of America.
For information, address St. Martin's Publishing Group,
120 Broadway, New York, NY 10271.

www.stmartins.com

Library of Congress Cataloging-in-Publication Data

Names: Greene, Kris, author.
Title: The reckoning / Kris Greene.
Description: First edition. | New York : St. Martin's Griffin, 2019. |
    Series: A dark storm novel ; 3
Identifiers: LCCN 2019019292 | ISBN 9780312943707 (paperback) |
    ISBN 9781429987011 (ebook)
Subjects: | BISAC: FICTION / Fantasy / Contemporary. | GSAFD:
    Fantasy fiction.
Classification: LCC PS3607.R4527 R43 2019 | DDC 813/.6—dc23
LC record available at https://lccn.loc.gov/2019019292

Our books may be purchased in bulk for promotional, educational,
or business use. Please contact your local bookseller or the Macmillan
Corporate and Premium Sales Department at 1-800-221-7945,
extension 5442, or by e-mail at
MacmillanSpecialMarkets@macmillan.com.

First Edition: November 2019

10 9 8 7 6 5 4 3 2 1

THE RECKONING

PROLOGUE

Gina had never considered herself a pretty girl. She was short with frizzy hair and a nose that needed a little off the end, and she was one cookie shy of being fat. So when she drew the attentions of a man like Sal, she was totally taken aback. With long, dark hair and rugged good looks, he was her dream man, and she knew she loved him from the first time she laid eyes on him. She vowed to follow him to the end of the world if he asked, but to him, the end of the world was a seedy motel on the west side of town.

They had barely crossed the threshold before Sal was on her. He placed his mouth over hers and tried to inhale all the breath from her body. He worked his way to her neck and began to plant kisses on it. His kissing had turned into him sucking on her skin so hard that she was sure it would leave a mark. She was about to tell him to take it easy, when she felt a sharp pinch. She tried to push Sal away, but his mouth was locked firmly onto her throat. Her body danced some-where between pleasure and pain as Sal continued to ravage her neck. When he came up for air, Gina saw that his mouth was smeared with what looked like blood . . . her blood.

Gina tried to scream, but Sal clamped his hand over her mouth. "Shut up, you stupid whore," he barked. His head whipped around, his eyes nervously searching. His gaze landed on the chair near the writing desk. Something was off about it, but he couldn't figure out what. Suddenly it hit him. It wasn't the chair, but the shadow it cast. It was facing the wrong direction.

Moving out of fear and reflex, Sal darted out of the way just before a wave of shadow crashed against the wall where he had been standing. Gina wasn't so lucky. When the inky shadow rolled back, there was nothing left of the girl but a mummified corpse with its face locked in a horrified expression. Sal took one look at Gina and knew immediately what he was dealing with . . . a shadow demon. From the looks of what was left of Gina it wasn't just any shadow demon either. It was one of the nastier ones who could cross between the mortal realm and the shadows at will. Sal leapt for the window, but before he could make it to freedom, he found him-self bound from ankle to neck in shadows. The tendrils dragged him across the room and pinned him upside down against the wall. Sal watched helplessly as the darkness reared up and the formless shape began to coagulate into the silhou-ette of a man. It was like a statue of complete darkness and the only signs of life were the glowing red eyes.

"Hello, Sal." The shadow greeted him in a voice that made the fresh blood running through Sal's veins run cold. This wasn't just a shadow demon, it was the shadow master himself.

"Moses," Sal croaked.

"There is no escape from the darkness," a voice to Sal's left said. Sal hadn't noticed him the first time, but he was sitting on the bed, watching through eyes as black as the shadows that bound Sal to the wall. He had oily black hair that hung down past his shoulders and ruggedly handsome features. One of the worn motorcycle boots he wore rested on the motel room's waste basket, rocking it back and forth. Dressed in a black leather jacket and tattered jeans, he looked like a rock star, but the thing resting across his lap was no musical instrument. It was a four-foot blade that looked as if it had been charred along the edges.

Even from across the room, Sal could feel the enchantment on the blade. Sal was no expert on demonology, but everyone knew the cursed blade Poison, and the demon who wielded it. His name was Riel. He wasn't just a war demon, but *the* war demon. As the legends went, Riel had whispered into the ears of thousands of kings and generals over the centuries, sparking some of the bloodiest wars in the history of the world. Finally realizing what he was up against, Sal had to swallow the ball of fear that was trying to force its way from his mouth like bile.

"This has got to be a mistake. You've got the wrong guy," Sal said.

Riel approached, carrying the waste basket with him. He placed it on the floor and looked at Sal. "No, I think we have the right guy, Salvatore Gangi. Or do you still go by the title: the Butcher?"

It had been a long time since Sal had heard that name, and the sound of it rolling off the war demon's tongue made his freshly warmed blood run cold. When he was still a mortal, he had earned the title *the Butcher* during WWII. Sal had been a medical officer in the Italian Army and member of the Nazi party. Sal was sadistic and took his pleasure in the torturing of Jewish prisoners. When he was done with his victims, he would cut up their bodies like chops or other meats and have them cooked and fed to privileged prisoners, the Jews who pledged their allegiance to the Nazis in exchange for preferential treatment. Sal and his men would watch in amusement as the traitors cannibalized their own. The only reason Sal was able to escape the hangman's noose was because he was made a vampire right before the Germans were defeated, and his comrades were put to death for crimes against humanity.

"Your kind holds no secrets from one who is praised as a god of war," Riel continued. "Fear not, Salvatore. For your sins, I have come to offer you absolution. The children of the fallen will help to usher in a new age, the age of *demons*."

"The elders have spoken, and everyone from the house of Gehenna knows that we're sitting this one out. Even if I wanted to serve you, I can't." Sal made one last attempt to negotiate with the demon.

Riel threw his head back and laughed. "My friend, you've placed too much value on yourself. We don't want you to serve, we want you to bleed." He drew his blade back to strike, but Moses stopped him.

"No." The shadow master intervened before Riel could deliver the fatal strike. "Slay him with the cursed blade and his body and blood become tainted and no good to us. The shadows will extract what is needed."

Moses held a palm out and slowly began to close his hand. There was a loud cracking sound as the shadows that had bound Sal's legs constricted, snapping them like twigs. Sal howled in pain as the shadows continued rolling over his helpless body, tightening, breaking bones, and squeezing him like a tube of toothpaste. Blood poured from Sal's mouth first, then his nose, and finally his eyes and ears, filling the waste basket below. When Sal was almost completely drained, Moses made a dismissive gesture, and the shadows tossed what was left of the vampire onto the bed.

Riel stalked over to the bed where Sal lay. The vampire's body was little more than a twisted bag of bones, but he was still alive. His eyes betrayed the hatred that was in his heart, but every bone in his body was broken, preventing him from acting on it. "For your sacrifice, I will make sure your name is forever carried in songs of celebration when the true masters of this world rise to reclaim it. All thanks to your blood, fallen one." He took his blade and nicked the back of Sal's hand. "May Poison's sweet kiss carry you into the afterlife."

Within seconds, the small cut on the back of Sal's hand began to heal. The wound had almost knitted itself closed when Sal felt fire shoot through his hand. The skin around the wound began to blacken and rot, eating away at his hand. The infection went up his arm and spread through his entire body, devouring flesh and soul. By the time the dark magic was done, there was nothing left of Sal but a motorcycle jacket covered in ash.

· CHAPTER ONE ·

Gabriel hit the murky sewer water with a splash. He reflexively opened his mouth from the impact and the filthy water flooded in. When he broke the surface of the water, he spat and sneezed in an attempt to remove the foul murk from his nose and mouth, but the stink remained. He grasped the edge of the walkway and pulled himself from the stale water, wet and smelling like a garbage truck. The too-tight burlap pants he had *borrowed* were already uncomfortable to wear, but now that they were soaked, it was ten times worse. He longed for his normal garb, a sweatshirt and jeans, but he'd abandoned them several hours prior for a more inconspicuous outfit, considering where his night would take him. If his friends at school could see him dressed like a character in a Shakespearean play, it would be one more thing to ridicule him about, but being laughed at was the least of his problems.

For as long as he could remember, Gabriel Redfeather had

always had shit luck. His parents had died mysteriously in a fire, which landed him in the care of his eccentric grandfather. The elder, who simply went by *Redfeather,* was a retired professor who spent the twilight of his years studying things that seemed to make no sense to anyone but him. Redfeather would keep his grandson, Gabriel, up to all hours, feeding his curiosity for the supernatural with his stories of things that had branded him a lunatic among his colleagues. At the end of each tale, he would always remind Gabriel that monsters were real but couldn't hurt him. A few days prior, Gabriel discovered a hard truth; his grandfather was a liar. Monsters were real and trying their best to hurt him.

In the blink of an eye, he had gone from a less-than-popular bookworm to a suspect in the death of his two best friends, and on the shit list of a very powerful demon. There was a bounty on Gabriel's head, and every creature of the night in the tristate area was gunning to collect, all because of the thing that had bound itself to his soul and the girl who handed it to him.

Thinking of DeMona brought Gabriel back to the reason he had willingly jumped back into a hole he had only narrowly escaped a few minutes prior. DeMona hadn't made it, which meant the goblins had her. They were outnumbered and out-muscled, as the goblins had swarmed the tunnel. Anything that hadn't made it out of that hole probably wouldn't, but he couldn't leave her behind.

Gabriel rolled to his feet, trident at the ready, prepared to once again do battle with the fierce goblins, but there was no sign of his enemy. In fact, there was no sign of anyone. It was as if someone or something had driven the goblins away. His gaze swept the tunnel, searching for his traveling companion. He spotted her a few yards down, kneeling on the ground. She looked beaten to shit, but she was still alive. Gabriel took a step toward DeMona, and the trident pulsed in his hand, sending a cold sense of dread up his arm. It was then that his gaze picked up on what he hadn't seen at first: DeMona wasn't alone.

Crouching in front of her, partially out of his view, was a woman . . . or what he assumed was a woman. It was hard to tell from the bulky gold armor and barrel-like shoulders. When the thing kneeling before DeMona looked up, Gabriel saw the spine of bone running up both sides of its forehead and the unnatural glow to its eyes. His mind screamed *demon*, and he rushed to help his friend. Halfway into his battle charge, he paused and a dumbstruck look crossed his face.

The demon's face began to wriggle and transform. The yellowish scales on her exposed flesh faded, leaving behind smooth olive skin. Her fangs retracted behind two perfectly bowed lips that were the color of rose pedals and her semi-blocked jaw rounded to a tender curve. When the horns receded back into her skull, her dark hair fanned around her face, a face that was nearly a mirror double of DeMona's. All Gabriel could do was blink to make sure his eyes weren't playing tricks on him.

DeMona wasn't sure what she was feeling, but it wasn't pleasant. Now that the fight was over, her adrenaline was bleeding off, and she was beginning to feel the aches in her limbs. The inside of her stomach did flip-flops, and she wasn't sure if she would be able to hold down what little food she did have in her stomach. Waves rolled under her skin as her body danced between two forms, one of peace and the other of war.

For what seemed like an eternity, her eyes remained locked on the woman standing across from her. Looking at the woman was like looking into a mirror. They both had the same beautiful features, dark hair, and tanned skin, but DeMona was younger and looked less battle-worn than her double. The most striking resemblance had to be the eyes, both sets shone with the unnatural moonlight that was the mark of their kind, the Valkrin. Though she could see her double clearly in the dimly lit tunnel, her mind was telling her it was impossible. It couldn't be her mother, not after what she'd done to their family.

"DeMona," Mercy said, extending her hand, "baby, it's Mommy."

"Don't . . . you . . . dare." DeMona's voice was heavy, and her words measured. Her two forms had finally finished their debate, and war had won over peace. Long talons extended from where her fingertips had been, and her shoulders broadened.

"Sweetie, I know you have so many questions, and if you'd just let me explain—" Mercy began, but was cut off when DeMona leapt to her feet.

DeMona was a ball of emotion. Her mind whirled with thoughts of how her mother had abandoned them, and her father's murder, and she snapped, "He died because of you." She lashed out twice, leaving eight slashes across Mercy's face, but the wounds healed just as quickly as they'd come, which only infuriated DeMona more. She raised her hand for another strike, but Mercy caught her arm in midswing. DeMona came around with the other talon, and Mercy stopped that strike easier than the first one. DeMona was stronger than most humans and some supernatural beings, but she was no match for her mother.

Still holding DeMona's arms, Mercy rose and regarded her daughter, the piece of her she had left behind. She saw so much of Edward's kind spirit in her, but she also saw the rage. Their race thrived on war and anger; it was in their genetic make-up. DeMona may have had a human father, but she was all Valkrin, like her mother. Mercy thought of what her daughter must've had to endure trying to live in two worlds with no one to guide her, and it broke her. There were no words that Mercy could find to mend her daughter's broken heart, so she did what came natural and hugged her.

"Let me go." DeMona struggled against her mother, but not enough to break free. She was resentful, but being in her mother's arms was the closest she had come to being at peace since she left. "How could you just leave us like that?"

"I am so sorry, DeMona." Mercy sobbed into her hair. "I swear if there had been any other way, I'd have never left my family behind." Mercy continued consoling her daughter until she remembered the human. When she noticed the trident in his hand, she recoiled and bared her fangs. Though she had never laid eyes on it, she knew what it was, and the tale behind it and its twisted master, the Bishop.

Several centuries prior, a mystic storm had torn a rift in the veil that separated the worlds of men and monsters. It was called the Dark Storm. It marked the beginning of what would be known as the Seven-Day Siege, a war between hell and earth. With the demon horde threatening to enslave humanity, the world once again needed heroes, and the church provided them with one—Bishop Michael Francisco. He was chosen to lead the secret order of the Knights of Christ into battle against the demons, armed with one of the church's most closely guarded artifacts, the Trident of Heaven.

The weapon was powerful indeed, and decimated the dark forces, but the Nimrod's services came at a price. The temptation of commanding power of that magnitude was overwhelming, even for those as devout as the Bishop and the knights he led into battle. The corruption started with him, but soon spread through his ranks, and he was eventually betrayed by his second-in-command, a knight named Titus, and struck down with the weapon he had wielded so faithfully. He sought to claim the trident as its own, but the Nimrod was not ready to part with the Bishop, and instead of letting his soul pass to the afterlife, it consumed it before turning on knights and demons alike. In the end, it was a young knight called Redfeather who was able to bring the trident under control and end the Seven-Day Siege. For centuries it was said that the trident, and the soul trapped with it, drifted through time and space waiting for the day when it would once again be commanded by its true master, the Bishop.

Mercy bared her fangs and stepped between her daughter and the weapon, prepared to either fight or die to protect her daughter.

"No, he's a friend." DeMona touched her mother's hand, and it seemed to soothe her. "This is Gabriel Redfeather."

Mercy scoffed. "So, this is the fool who woke the Nimrod and set the wheels of the apocalypse in motion?"

"Hey, it's not like I did it on purpose, so I'd appreciate it if you and everybody else got off my case for a little while," Gabriel said heatedly.

Don't let your tongue cost you your head, young hunter. The Valkrin are quick to anger and quicker to murder, the Bishop whispered into his ear. The soul captured in the trident had been silent until then, but being in such close proximity to the demon unnerved him.

Mercy's head cocked to one side, and she gave Gabriel a quizzical look. "It's true what they say, isn't it?"

Gabriel abandoned his conversation and looked up at her. "It depends on what they're saying."

Mercy moved closer to get a better look at the trident, but didn't dare go within arm's reach. "They say the Bishop's spirit still lives, and secretly orchestrates events through those whom the Nimrod chooses as his puppets."

"I'm nobody's puppet!" Gabriel declared.

"Are you trying to convince me or yourself?" Mercy asked.

DeMona stepped between them. "Back off, Mercy. When the shit hit the fan, Gabriel was there for me, which is more than I can say for you."

Mercy sighed deeply. "DeMona, I know you're upset—"

DeMona cut her off. "*Upset* is an understatement."

"Fine, you're *angry.* You have every right to be, but you have to understand that I did what I had to do to protect you." She took DeMona's face in her hands, and the girl didn't resist. "To your father and me, you were the most beautiful thing we had ever laid eyes on. To the Valkrin, you'd have been an abomination, flawed and weak because of your human blood. Had the Valkrin come to claim me, instead of me going willingly, can you imagine what they would've done to you?"

DeMona pulled away. "No worse than they've already done, by killing my father and mother," she spat.

Mercy's nostrils flared at the statement, but she remained calm. "We Valkrin are born warriors, and to die in battle is the highest honor bestowed upon our kind. When the call to arms goes out, *all* Valkrin are bound by blood and tradition to answer. To ignore the call is to die in shame, and trust me, my sisters wouldn't have stopped until we were all dead."

Mercy's confession touched DeMona. She could feel tears welling, but wouldn't allow them to fall. "We could've fought them together."

Mercy shook her head. "Little one, you still have so much to learn about what we are. The enemies of the Valkrin do not fight, they *die!* By leaving behind the ones I loved the most, I spared you the life the Valkrin would've condemned you to."

DeMona could feel her anger wavering, so she held onto it with everything she had. "Are we supposed to kiss and make up now?" she asked sarcastically.

"DeMona, I don't expect you to forgive me, but I expect you to understand." Mercy was calm, but her daughter could feel the anger rolling off her. DeMona was pushing it.

The trident pulsed in Gabriel's hand, warning him of danger. His eyes immediately flashed to the dark tunnel. He couldn't see the goblins, but he could feel them coming. There were more of them this time. "I think this is a conversation that should be had outside this tunnel, ladies," Gabriel suggested.

Mercy was about to snap at Gabriel for interrupting but her ears picked up what the trident was trying to warn him of. She couldn't be sure, but by the sounds of their footfalls, there were over a dozen of them. "The human is right. We'd better go before they get here." She sprang effortlessly up through the hole leading to the upper level.

DeMona shook her head at her mother's slur and gave Gabriel an apologetic look. She tried to mimic her mother and leap up through the hole, but she fell short. Mercy's firm hand grabbed her about the wrists and pulled her effortlessly up. DeMona was surprised at how strong her mother actually was, and it showed on her face.

"When you mature and come into your full Valkrin strength, you'll be able to do that and so much more," Mercy told her.

"Maybe, unless my human blood stunts my growth," De-Mona said cruelly. "Let's go, Gabriel," she called over her shoulder and brushed past her mother to regroup with the others.

"Your human friend is wasting time." Mercy was on her heels. She made no attempt to hide her mounting irritation with her daughter.

"He's coming, so why don't you relax?" DeMona snapped.

"Because I don't like sitting around waiting to be slaugh-tered by the goblin horde. We must keep moving."

"You've got a lot of nerve, popping up after all this time and trying to give me orders. I've been doing fine without you this long," DeMona said.

There was a loud hissing which caused mother and daughter to turn around. They couldn't see him at first because he was hiding in the shadows, but it didn't take their Valkrin eyes long to pierce the veil. He was small by goblin standards, standing no taller than a small human child. His skin was a sickly shade of green, and his teeth were like little yellow needles. With pointed ears and a pair of useless leathery wings on his back, he looked more like an overgrown bat than a gob-lin prince.

"Demon!" Gilchrist tried to press himself farther into the shadows. "Kill us all, the Valkrin has come to do. Slay her! Slay her!" Gilchrist shouted.

Before DeMona could explain, Cristobel and Jak, the dwarves she had been traveling with, came to investigate. Cristobel was plump, with jovial blue eyes and brown hair, while Jak was lean with blond hair. Both dwarves were beard-less, the final mark of shame the goblins had laid upon them when they stormed the Iron Mountains and stripped the dwarves of their home and their freedom.

"By the gods!" Jak drew his twin blades when he saw Mercy. Cristobel was at his side, battle-axe drawn and poised to strike. They surrounded Mercy, prepared to engage in a battle both knew they had no chance of winning. Fighting a goblin was one thing, but this was a Valkrin, and the Valkrin didn't die easily.

DeMona tried to shout an explanation, but Jak had already made his move. Jak was incredibly quick, but the speed at which Mercy moved was unbelievable. His two blades clanked harmlessly to the ground, just before the back of her hand met with his chin, sending him flying to the other side of the chamber. Cristobel swung his axe, but Mercy easily side-stepped it, and grabbed the shaft. She yanked it from Cristobel's hand with so much force that she was sure to have broken at least one of his fingers. Mercy regarded the axe as if it were a child's toy, before tossing it to the side and turning her attention toward Cristobel.

Mercy shook her head sadly at the frightened dwarf. "So, these are the souls who were expected to be trusted with my only daughter's life, on your fool's mission into the pits of hell?" She lifted him by the front of his shirt. "Pathetic."

"Mother, stop it!" DeMona shouted. She tried to pull her mother's arm to free Cristobel, but she might as well have been a fly buzzing around the Valkrin.

Mercy cast an irritated glance over her shoulder at

her daughter before she dropped Cristobel roughly to the ground. "DeMona, you can't hope to stand against Titus with a mismatched band of misfits and a bumbling human, who will likely destroy himself before he gets within a stone's throw of the favorite son."

DeMona helped Cristobel off the ground, then moved to check on Jak. "We may not be much, but we're the only shot the world has got at this point. Now, are you going to help us or keep criticizing my friends?" She stood in front of her withered group like their champion. Even Gilchrist inched closer to stand with her.

Mercy let out a deep sigh. "Fine, DeMona. I will lay down my life to protect you, but I cannot guarantee anyone else's safety." Her eyes swept the group.

"Fair enough," DeMona agreed.

"Good, now let's be away from here before the goblins rally back in force," Mercy told them.

"Where is Gabriel?" Cristobel asked.

In answer to his question, there was the loud crashing of waves coming from somewhere below, followed by a geyser of water spilling up through the hole in the floor.

"Let's go, Redfeather," Gabriel heard DeMona shout down through the hole.

"Right behind you," Gabriel told her. He was about to leap for the hole when the trident began pulsing intensely, warning him of danger. He moved just as a small arrow whistled past him and embedded itself in the wall behind him. His eyes went to the darkened tunnel. He couldn't see the goblins, but he knew they were there, inching ever closer, their numbers growing. If they continued running, it would only be a matter of time before the goblins overran them, so he would hold them off and try to buy his companions some time.

The Bishop snickered. *Noble, but foolish.*

"So what do you propose we do, keep running until the goblins eventually mow us down?" Gabriel snapped.

For as much as watching you slaughtered by these savages would amuse me, I still have need of you, hunter. Stumbling upon great power is simple; understanding how to manipulate it to serve you is not so simple. Did you expect it to tell you its secrets willingly? the Bishop taunted.

"And what would you have me do, interrogate a pitchfork?"

The trident was forged to serve the Master of Storms. Thy will be done, the Bishop told him before going silent again.

"What does that mean?" Gabriel demanded, but the Bishop didn't answer.

There was a sickening screech coming from somewhere down the tunnel. The goblins were almost on them. A flurry of arrows pierced the darkness, headed straight for Gabriel. He barely had time to raise the trident to deflect them. One arrow went rogue and crashed into the ceiling of the cavern, dislodging some of the stones. The debris hit the murky water and splashed Gabriel, soaking him further and adding to his already mounting frustration. In anger he drew the trident back, prepared to cast it down the tunnel but froze when the Bishop's words took root.

Yes, Master of Storms. And lightning isn't the only thing storms can manipulate.

The first of the goblin reinforcements spilled from the tunnel, some on foot and some on the backs of the mutated hairless rats that patrolled the tunnels, all with murder on their minds. The nastiest of the lot was a mountain of a beast with a tiny pin head and one eye. Clutched in one of his monstrous hands was a club carved from stone. When he hit the wall with it, the whole cavern shook.

Gabriel approached the lip of the cavern floor, just above the river of sludge. "If I'm wrong"—he looked at the goblin charging him with the stone club—"I guess it won't matter." He held the trident out over the river and concentrated. When nothing happened, Gabriel got frustrated.

He heard the Bishop speak. *There is a fine line between weapon and master, which side do you stand on?*

Gabriel held the trident in both hands and focused. The murky water finally began to bubble and crash over the lip of the cavern in small waves, but it wasn't enough, so he tried harder. As Gabriel pushed, he could feel something pushing back. It was as if the Nimrod was fighting him for control. With a grunt, he gave it everything he had and felt the barrier shatter.

A gust of air swept through the tunnel and washed over Gabriel, before sending a ripple through the murky water. Chills ran up Gabriel's arms as if he could feel the flow of the water in his veins. Holding the trident with one hand, he began turning it in a counterclockwise circle, as if he were stirring a caldron. The water responded by spinning into a violent swirl in time with his motions. Gabriel stretched his free hand and lifted it slowly, bringing the water up with it. The sludge had spun into a tight tube of liquid fury, and with a thrust of his hand, Gabriel released it on the goblins.

The recoil from the typhoon Gabriel had released was so strong that it threw him into the wall, knocking the wind out of him. He watched through hazy eyes as the water washed through the tunnel and over the goblins. His ears were filled with their dying screams as the water flooded the tunnel. He tried to climb to higher ground, but the rising tide knew neither friend nor foe and swallowed him as well. Beneath the murky water, he could see the bodies of his enemies, churning helplessly in the vortex. He felt something bump into his back and thought it was the cavern wall, until he turned around and saw the beady eyes set within the abnormally small head staring back at him. The goblin wrapped its massive hands around Gabriel's face and began to apply pressure.

When the goblin grabbed Gabriel, he was caught off guard and dropped the Nimrod. Before he could recover it, massive hands enclosed his face. Pain shot through his head as the goblin tightened his grip and began the process of crushing his skull. He kicked and punched at the goblin, but was no match for its brutish strength. His life began to flash before his eyes, as he knew he was living his final moments. He could see his parents' proud faces the first time he'd ridden his bike across the tightrope. He could smell Katy's conditioner the day she helped him pick his books up off the floor outside their global studies class. He thought of his grandfather, and how he had failed them all.

"No!" Gabriel screamed into the goblin's hands. The force of his voice was like a small explosion, and he was free of the goblin's grip. A few feet away he could see the goblin disoriented, but still more than willing to continue the fight. He shot forward toward Gabriel like a torpedo. Instinctively, Gabriel raised his hands to prepare for the impact, and the trident appeared. Unable to stop his lunge, the goblin impaled himself on the points of the trident, and there was a flash of lightning under the water and white light began to pour from every hole in the goblin's body. When the light died, the goblin was a petrified shell, which began to sink like a stone, taking Gabriel and the trident with him.

Gabriel tugged feverishly at the trident but couldn't dislodge it, and they were sinking fast. He could feel the burning in his lungs from trying to hold his breath for so long and knew if he didn't do something quick, he would drown. Gabriel focused his will and forced it into the Nimrod. The trident responded by releasing a surge of energy, but it was uncontrolled and exploded, propelling him upward. There was a brief window during his ascent when Gabriel was free of the water and able to suck in the air he had desperately needed, only to have it knocked out of him a few seconds later when his back slammed into the ceiling, then crashed to the floor. He looked up and saw shapes moving around him. More goblins, no doubt. Gabriel flexed his hand, trying to call for the trident, but it didn't materialize. Even if it had, he was in too much pain to lift it, let alone defend himself. He closed his eyes and prepared to accept his end.

Instead of the tear of goblin teeth and claws, Gabriel felt a leathery hand slap him across the face. His eyes popped open, and he saw DeMona leaning over him, scowling.

"We're supposed to be saving the world and you're napping?" DeMona asked sarcastically.

Mercy brushed past her daughter, reached down, grabbed Gabriel by the front of his shirt, and snatched him to his feet. "Can you walk?"

Gabriel tested his weight on his legs. "Yes."

"Good, then keep moving. We've still got some ground to cover if we're to reach the heart of the Iron Mountains in time to rescue your people." She kicked Gilchrist. "Lead on, rodent."

Gilchrist bared his fangs at Mercy. "Like you very much, I don't."

Mercy leaned in and drew her lips back so he could see her fangs, which were like thick pointed canines. "Hate me very much, you will, if you don't get us inside the mountain."

Gilchrist muttered something and walked off. The rest of the group fell in step behind him. They all made it a point to keep a safe distance from the elder Valkrin, including DeMona. Every so often, she would cast a scornful glance at her mother, but avoided making eye contact. Eventually, it was Gabriel who fell in step beside her.

"So, you're DeMona's mother?" he asked, for lack of a better way to start a conversation.

Mercy cut her eyes to him. "I should hope your battle skills are as sharp as your knack for stating the obvious."

"I'm sorry. I didn't mean any offense. It's just that when she told me stories of you, I didn't quite picture you to be like"— he hesitated—"well, like this." He motioned toward her armor and sword.

"And what did you expect, human? Was I to be some happy housewife, wearing an apron and a plastic smile?" Her tone was sarcastic. "Make no mistake, human, I am a Valkrin, born and bred for battle, regardless of my flaws." Her eyes involuntarily went to DeMona.

"Was it hard?" Gabriel asked.

"Was what hard?"

"Leaving them."

Mercy stopped walking. Her moonlit eyes bore into Gabriel, and he took a cautionary step back in case he had offended her. Her lips twisted into a scowl. "I've taken over one thousand lives since I first learned to use claw and sword and have never felt anything for the poor souls I cast into the abyss, but leaving my husband and daughter shattered me."

"I can only imagine."

Her eyes narrowed. Mercy held her hand up for Gabriel to see that her delicate fingers were now daggers. "To have your child stripped from you is like having someone reach into your chest and tear your heart out while it's still beating. Can you truly imagine my pain, human?"

"I'm sorry," Gabriel offered sincerely. He decided to change the subject. "Mercy, you've just come from the mountain. Have you seen my grandfather?"

Mercy hesitated. "The last I'd heard he was alive, but that was before you and your friends busted in here and announced yourselves. Now, there's no telling." She noticed the worried expression cross Gabriel's face. "Gabriel, dead or alive, it doesn't change what must be done if you're to save this world. We are at war, and all soldiers must accept death as a part of war."

"I'm no soldier," he said.

She turned on him. "You're right, the moment you woke the Nimrod and bonded with it, you became a general, and if any of you plan to live like a general, I suggest you start acting like one." Mercy stormed off.

Heavy is the head of he who wears the crown, the Bishop whispered.

"Why don't you be quiet?" he barked at the tattoo on his arm.

Gabriel looked over and noticed everyone was watching the exchange between him and the Bishop. They looked frightened and weary, but he knew that down to the last man, they would continue fighting . . . they would fight for him, their leader. Gabriel had considered himself a failure for his entire life, but he would not fail them. They had put their faith and their lives in his hands, and he would see them through to the end, even if he died in the process.

· CHAPTER TWO ·

Asha stood with a look somewhere between shock and irritation splashed across her chocolate face. Her auburn eyes burned behind hooded lids while her lips were twisted into a scowl. Her slender fingers clenched and unclenched, flicking off light sparks of magic, but she dared not call her full power with the deck stacked against her and no plan.

Standing a few feet away from her were two women, both beautiful and both dangerous. At first glance, the girls could be mistaken for twins, but upon closer inspection you'd notice Lisa was more muscular and slightly taller than Lane, who was holding the gun. At one point, Lisa and Lane had been the closest things to family that Asha had left, but that night, they stood on opposite sides of a double cross and a loaded machine gun.

"You had better think about what you're about to do before this gets to the point of no return," Asha warned, looking from one girl to the other.

"I think we're already at that point, Asha. Dutch says we are to bring you in, but he wasn't real specific on whether you had to still be breathing or not. Now, we can do this the easy way"—Lane chambered a round into the machine gun—"or the hard way."

Asha's jaw tightened. "You girls know me better than anyone, so you know there's only one way to do this."

"I figured you'd say that." Lane smiled and depressed the trigger. She squeezed off a quick burst, but Asha was already leaping behind a car. Lane turned the machine gun on the car and opened fire.

Asha crouched behind the car with her eyes squeezed shut and her hands over her ears, as glass rained on her head from the shattered car windows. Never in a million years would Asha have thought Lisa and Lane would've ever betrayed her. Lisa and Lane were the only two witches in the coven who hadn't shunned her for the sins of her mother and the tainted blood she carried. They had taken the oath at the same time, not only swearing fidelity to the coven, but love for each other. It was a bond the trio had sworn would last even through death, but just like all the others, Lisa and Lane had betrayed her, and now they would feel her wrath.

"Azuma, attend your mistress!" Asha called.

The small monkey leapt onto the top of the car Asha was hiding behind and faced the attacking witches. He stood just over a foot tall with brownish fur and a ruddy pink face. He was Asha's familiar, a magical conduit and guardian. Azuma leapt off the car and charged, transforming as he went. By the time he reached the witch holding the machine gun, he had grown into a nine-foot silver gorilla with horns jutting from his head.

"Destroy them," Asha commanded.

Eager to do his mistress's bidding, Azuma attacked. Lane tried to bring the machine gun around, but Azuma knocked it away. She raised her hands to cast a spell, but Azuma was prepared and grabbed her about the wrist, binding her hands. He picked Lane up so they were at eye level and roared, raining rank spittle in her face.

Lane rubbed her face on her bicep to wipe the moisture away. "Sounds good, but here's my counteroffer." She opened her mouth, and from it flew a thick, silver liquid that coated Azuma's face. She took the moment of the familiar's confusion to kick off his chest and free herself from his grasp.

Lisa rushed to help her sister. She barely missed one of the gorilla's massive flailing paws. Running low to the ground and circling Azuma's legs, Lisa spit webs of pure white from her mouth, ensnaring his ankles. When the gorilla tried to move, he fell over like a ton of bricks, rattling the ground and setting off several car alarms. When he was down, the sisters bound him in a cocoon of white and silver silk.

"You must think you're the only witch with a familiar, Asha," Lane called to her.

"Come, sister, and watch your pet die," Lisa added. She called her power and approached Azuma, ready to deliver the death stroke. There was a whistling sound. Something crashed into the street a few feet away, cracking it. The girls watched in shock, as something sped toward them like a torpedo, tearing a path in the concrete and exploding in a spray of debris, knocking them back. Through the cloud of dust stepped a stocky man, who was tall and had red hair and a shaggy beard of the same color. In his hand, still covered with dust from the concrete, was a jeweled war hammer.

Morgan twirled the hammer in his hand as if it were weightless and regarded the stunned witches. "That monkey is a pain in the ass, of this you can be sure." Faint traces of his native Ireland bled into his accent. "But he amuses me, so I think I'd like to keep him alive for a while, if it's all the same to you."

"Mind your business, stranger. This is coven business and no concern of yours," Lane spat.

"And this is where I would beg to differ. The witch and her pet are under my protection, so that makes them my concern." His grip tightened around the handle of the hammer. "If you lasses leave now, I promise not to spank you for being naughty."

Lisa stepped forward, blade in one hand and a spell in the other. "Too bad, because I kinda like spankings." She charged Morgan, chanting the proper incantation, and released the spell.

Answering to her magic, pieces of loose stone rose from the ground and sprayed Morgan's face. Lisa brought her blade around and swung it at Morgan's exposed neck with everything she had. When the blade made contact, it broke and the point landed helplessly at her feet. She looked in bewilderment and saw the last few remnants of the rocks absorbed into Morgan's skin, which was now tinted a marble hue.

"What are you?" she gasped.

"When I figure it out completely, you'll be the first I share the secret with." Morgan hit her with a right cross. He pulled the punch, but his stone fist still hit Lisa with enough force to send her flying across the street and into a parked car.

Lane tried to blindside Morgan, but her feet were swept out from under her, sending her face-first to the ground. She looked over her shoulder and saw Asha in a defensive crouch. "So, you've finally decided to come out and fight your own battle?" She quickly got off the ground. "Good."

The two witches circled each other, careful not to waste magic unnecessarily, because they both knew it wouldn't be an easy fight. It was unreal to Asha how someone who had been like a sister to her was now trying to kill her. She wanted to wake up and realize it had all been a bad dream, but the roundhouse kick Lane threw at her head let her know it was real. Asha faked a kick at Lane then came around and hit her with a left. Lane sprang right back with a series of combinations, flustering Asha. Lane tried to grab Asha's face, but she caught her hand and kept it from making contact. Asha could feel the magic pouring from Lane's hand, and she knew the spell she was trying to cast was a nasty one because Asha had taught it to her.

Asha twisted Lane's arm behind her back and kicked her, sending the witch stumbling forward and putting some distance between them. Morgan moved to help Asha, but she waved him away. "No, I can handle this," she told him and Morgan reluctantly backed off. "Lane, stop this before it gets out of hand." For as angry as Asha was, she still didn't really want to hurt her friend.

"You're not Dutch's favorite anymore, so your days of giving me orders are over," Lane informed her. She had always been secretly jealous of the sway Asha had over Dutch.

Lane launched at Asha, throwing a combination of punches, fists infused with deadly magic. Asha warded off the blows and hit Lane in the gut with a strong hook. When Lane doubled over, Asha followed with an uppercut and set Lane down in the street like a drunk. Frustrated, Lane jumped to her feet and prepared to attack again.

"I don't want to hurt you, Lane," Asha told her.

"And what makes you think you *can* hurt me?" Lane fired back. "Ever since we were novices, you've always been looked at as the strong one, the protector. You know how sick I got of hearing how great of a Mistress of the Hunt you'd be, and not so much as a mention of me or my sister? Can you imagine the ridicule we secretly endured for being two pure-blooded witches who would forever live in the shadows of a *mongrel?*" Lane knew as soon as the word left her mouth that she had gone too far, but she was caught in the heat of the moment and her feelings.

Asha winced as if she had just been slapped when Lane hurled the insult. *Mongrel* had been what some in the coven secretly called Asha since she was a little girl. She wasn't a pure blood witch, and they went out of their way to remind her of it every chance they got. Asha's mother had been a Voundon priestess of a long dead cult, who trafficked in dark magic. She was convicted of murdering a warlock, but her only real crime was falling in love with a married man who was willing to murder her and her unborn child to keep his secret from getting out. Asha's mother was put to death for the crime, and Asha was awarded to the Black Court as restitution. It was there she came under the instruction of Dutch, the Black King. Though Asha was afforded the same training as the pure witches of the coven, she was reminded every day of her impurities and the fact that she didn't belong.

Asha was hurt, but wouldn't give Lane the satisfaction of showing it. Instead, she simply spoke the words that would ultimately tell the tale. "When there is conflict between two witches of the same coven which cannot be resolved by words, let them be resolved by magic and blood." Asha was invoking one of the oldest rituals among the coven, a duel of magic.

Lane was hesitant in responding. She knew that the duels were to the death, and there could be no outside interference, which meant she was on her own. She looked from her sister, who was just stirring from her spill, to Asha, who was glaring at her smugly . . . challenging her, as she'd done when they were growing up. She was tired of living in Asha's shadow. "And may the blood spilled return to the earth from which it came to water the new things that will grow in place of those that have fallen," Lane answered the challenge.

"No!" Lisa shrieked. She knew Lane was a powerful spell caster, but no match for Asha. Ignoring her injuries, she made a mad dash toward Asha and Lane to try and stop the duel.

Morgan grabbed Lisa from behind and wrapped her in a bear hug. She opened her mouth to cast a spell, but he slapped his meaty hand over it. "No, you don't. This one will be a fair fight."

The two witches lunged at the same time, throwing blows infused with magic. Lane swung her hand like a claw at Asha's face, leaving a trail of faint green energy, representing the earth from which she drew her strength. Asha raised her hand to deflect the blow, sending off splatters of crimson energy which resembled blood. Lane tried her best to force her hands to make contact with Asha's face, but Asha held her about the wrist tightly. Lane was physically stronger than Asha so she tried to use her weight against her, but Asha went with it and Lane stumbled, leaving herself open for a roundhouse kick to the back that sent her stumbling forward. Lane roared in frustration and charged Asha again. This time, Asha simply stepped out of the way and punched Lane in the back of her head as she passed.

Asha shook her head sadly. "You blame me for you getting passed over, but it's your own fault. One of the key lessons we learn in the first circle is that emotions dilute the spell. You can't control your feelings, which is why you'll always be a second-rate spell caster." She chuckled.

"Let's see if you're still laughing when they're scrubbing your blood off this sidewalk." Lane reached behind her and produced the small handgun that Lisa had insisted she bring along, then set out to take Asha down. She'd initially been opposed to the idea of the weapon, but being on the receiving end of an ass-kicking, she was glad that she had it. It was against the rules of the duel to use weapons other than magic, but Lane didn't care about rules, she cared about winning.

Before Lane could get her finger anywhere near the trigger, Asha was on the move. She leapt to one side, flicking two small disks at Lane. At the same time Lane pulled the trigger, one of the disks kissed off the gun, knocking it out of her hand while the other whistled past her ear, just missing her face, before it swung back to Asha like a boomerang.

"Your aim is getting poor, Asha," Lane taunted.

"Is it?" Asha held the disk up. There was a faint smear of blood along its edge.

Lane nervously touched her hand to her ear and her fingertips came away bloody. It was a small scratch, but she knew it was all Asha needed. "No," Lane gasped.

"Yes." Asha smiled menacingly as she rubbed the disk between her palms, making sure to get a little of the blood on each hand. The blood began to glow as she called upon her greatest magic, the magic of her people. "As it was with my mother and her mother before her, the blood is the essence and our strength. She who I once called sister, I command you to bleed!"

Blood squirted in an arc from Lane's ear. She clamped her hand over the cut, but blood only spilled through her fingers and dripped down her arm. Lane frantically tried to stammer out a spell, but only got halfway through it before blood began to spill from her mouth too. Lane collapsed on the ground, thrashing and bleeding from every hole in her body.

"Stop it, you're killing her!" Lisa shouted. She snapped her head back into Morgan's jaw, catching him by surprise and causing him to loosen his grip enough for her to wriggle free. Blade in hand, she attacked Asha . . . or at least tried to. She got within three feet before her leg buckled, and she fell. Lisa clutched at her knee as if someone had set it on fire. When she moved her hand, she could see a bloodstain in the fabric that seemed to be spreading.

Asha turned to Lisa, auburn dreads clinging to her forehead from her sweat. "Those are some nasty scrapes you've got on your knee from your little spill. If I were you, I'd get them looked at before they get infected." She wrenched her hand, and Lisa's knee began to bleed heavier. It was torture for the sisters, but like sweet release for Asha.

Morgan saw the look on Asha's face and recognized it. He had seen it staring back at him in the mirror on more than a few occasions when he had first come into possession of the hammer. She was drunk with power and trying to climb further still into the bottle. "Asha, that's enough." He grabbed Asha's arm, and to his surprise, her skin was almost scalding to the touch.

"They wanted it like this, not me," Asha said in a low rasp. Her magic fed off her anger and seemed to grow stronger. She was exerting so much magical energy that though Morgan wasn't the target, standing in proximity to Asha drew a trickle of blood from his nose.

"Jesus on the cross." Morgan staggered backward, wiping the blood from his nose with the back of his hand.

Seeing Morgan's blood snapped Asha out of it. "By the Goddess." She looked at her still-glowing hands in horror.

"Are you okay?" She reached out to Morgan, but he took a step back.

"I'm fine," he lied, looking at the blood across the back of his hand. It was near impossible to hurt him when he used his gift to tap into earth or stone, but she had done so without even trying. The witch was far more dangerous than probably even she knew, and he made a mental note to speak to Jonas when they got back to the scrap yard.

"Morgan, it's never done that. I don't know what happened," Asha tried to explain.

"No worries, you can talk about it later. Right now, let's take our leave of this place and help the others." Morgan took a step toward their vehicle when he caught a flicker of movement. Without thinking, he tackled Asha and shielded her with his body, just as they were showered with bullets. The concrete was still coursing through his skin, so he was able to withstand the brunt of the assault, but the effects of the blood magic had weakened him. There was a pinch in his side, but he ignored it, crawling on his belly and dragging Asha behind a parked car.

"You're hurt." Asha noticed the blood on his shirt. "Let me see how bad it is." She reached for him, but he drew back.

"No, I'm okay." Morgan pressed his hand to the wound on his side.

"You're not okay. You're bleeding all over the place. Let me see the wound." Asha swatted his hand out of the way. Reluctantly, Morgan lifted his shirt and let her see his wound. The bullet had only grazed him, but it had opened a nasty gash on his side.

"It's not too bad, Red. I might know a spell—"

"You'll not be working any blood magic on me. I've seen what it can do." Morgan's grip on his hammer tightened.

Asha looked down at her hands then looked back up at him confidently. "There is no good or evil in the blood, only life and death. What you saw was death." She pressed her hand to his wound. It was hot, but soothing. When she removed her hand, the wound had stopped bleeding. "This is life." Their eyes met and something passed between them. Before either of them could figure out what it was, bullets ripped through the side of the car.

Asha spared a glance through one of the car's broken windows and saw Lisa. She looked like death, covered in blood and dragging her injured leg behind her uselessly, but her hands were working just fine, and in them, she held the machine gun she'd retrieved. "Don't run now." Lisa let loose another spray. "You're gonna pay for what you did to my sister, Asha!" She fired off another burst.

Asha waited for a pause in Lisa's ranting and shooting before popping up from behind the car. Lisa saw her at the same time Asha reared her hand back to hurl one of her disks, when suddenly everything went quiet. It was as if a vacuum had swept through and sucked out all the sound on the block. The streetlight blinked dark, and when it came back on, the whole scene had changed. When Asha saw the players who had joined in the game, it made her throat very, very dry.

Standing directly in front of Asha was an average height Asian man, with long hair and a tattoo that went from his eye to his jawline. If she remembered correctly, his name was Teko. His hands were clasped and held at eye level so Asha could see the katana blade he was holding. Her eyes slowly traveled down the blade, and she saw the blood dripping from it. She cast her eyes up and stared beyond him where Lisa stood, midstep. Her eyes were fierce and angry, her face twisted into a hateful scowl. Teko swung his blade dangerously close to Asha's face, before whipping it behind him and flicking blood on Lisa. Her body went one way, but her head went another when it fell from her shoulders and rolled to the curb, where it was stopped by a high-polished black shoe.

The man wearing the shoes was taller than most of his kind, but was only about five-eight, although his presence was that of someone physically larger. His skin was two shades darker than the night and seemed to swallow the light from the streetlamp. Pointed ears were barely exposed beneath a beautiful mane of waist-length hair that was such a deep shade of blue that it looked black at a glance. His name was Gilgamesh, last true prince of the dark elves, and heir to the throne of the Black Forest of Midland, but in the human world, he was simply known as Mesh, underboss and enforcer for the notorious Croft crime family.

"Have you all taken complete leave of your senses?" When Gilgamesh spoke, his voice seemed to come from everywhere at once. He kicked Lisa's head out of the way and walked to Asha. Violet eyes stared at her from beneath hooded black lids. "That's twice tonight you've spilled blood on my property without an invitation."

Morgan stepped up, hammer dangling at his side. "To be sure, we could all talk like nice folk without standing so close, can't we?"

"It's cool, Red. I know him . . . kind of." Asha gently pushed Morgan to the side and faced Gilgamesh on her own.

Gilgamesh's eyes drifted past Asha to the hammer in Morgan's hand. He knew what it was and where it came from, but what he didn't know was what it was doing there and how the redhead had come into possession of it. When Gilgamesh was finally able to tear his eyes away from the hammer, he turned them back to Asha. "I give you a pass, and you squander it?"

"Gilgamesh, I didn't mean to. They didn't leave me much choice. Dutch sent them to kill me," Asha admitted, figuring honesty was her best chance at not finding herself on the receiving end of Teko's blade.

Gilgamesh was surprised at the information, but did his best not to show it. It was said that Asha sat in high favor with the Black King, so what could make him place a bounty on her so suddenly? Then there was the fact that his uncle had gone to a meeting earlier that night and Dutch was also to attend. There was something definitely afoot, and Gilgamesh suddenly got an uneasy feeling in his stomach.

"Little witch, your troubles get more and more curious by the hour, don't they? I'll spare you . . . again, but I am curious to know why Dutch would want you dead so badly," Gilgamesh told her.

There was a wet coughing sound coming from where Lane still lay twitching faintly. Teko went over and checked her vitals. A grim expression crossed his face, and he shook his head sadly.

"Dispatch her then dump the body and meet me inside." Gilgamesh started toward the herb shop.

Teko raised his blade to end Lane's life, but Asha stopped him. "No, if her blood is to be spilled, I have to be the one to do it. I won the duel," Asha said with great sadness in her voice.

Teko looked at Gilgamesh, who simply nodded, letting him know it was okay. The Gammurai stepped back while Asha knelt over Lane.

There was so much blood that she had a hard time holding

her head, but she managed to get it onto her lap. Lane's eyes rolled back in her head, and her body jerked involuntarily. She was alive but clearly suffering. Asha drew her dagger. The blade was as black as coal and the handle carved from the bone of an infant, etched with magical ruins. It had been her mother's parting gift to her and the only thing she had to remember her by.

Asha leaned in and kissed Lane's forehead. With great sorrow in her heart, she placed the blade under Lane's chin. "I am so sorry it had to end like this," she whispered in her ear, not sure if the girl was coherent enough to hear or understand her. "May the blood spilled return to the earth from which it came to water the new things that will grow in place of those that have fallen." She cut Lane's throat and ended her suffering. When she stood, Gilgamesh was at her side.

"Murder in the heat of battle is a far different animal than doing it in cold blood, wouldn't you agree?" Gilgamesh grinned slyly.

Murdering her best friend rode Asha like a dark horse, so she took exception at Gilgamesh's remark. "Why don't you go fuck yourself?"

Enraged by her lack of respect, Gilgamesh grabbed Asha's arm and wrenched it to one side. "If I were you, I'd remember where I was." He motioned around at his domain.

Asha sighed. "I know where I am, and I'm too tired to give a shit. Now, either we're gonna get it on out here, or you're gonna get the hell out of our way so we can go help Rogue and the others."

Gilgamesh softened his stance a bit when hearing his friend Rogue's name. He and the mage had history. "Asha, were you and my starry-eyed friend out to lunch earlier when I said that this war has nothing to do with the dark elves? What care we if man and demon want to destroy each other?"

"You might want to care. People like Titus are parasites; their appetites know no bounds. When they have enslaved humanity and taken over this world, how long do you think it'll be before they start looking for other realms to conquer, maybe even yours?" Morgan pointed out.

Gilgamesh threw his head back and gave a throaty laugh. "We elves are the oldest of all races and one of the few who still thrive in the modern era. This is not by accident. We have seen control of worlds passed back and forth through blood and steel over a thousand times, yet we remain, because we take no personal stake in anything that does not affect the dark elves. Everything else is strictly business."

There were the sounds of footfalls in the distance. Teko reacted first, katana drawn, positioning himself between Gilgamesh and whatever was approaching. A figure spilled from the shadows. By its awkward and staggered approach, it appeared injured. As it came into view, Teko raised his blade to strike, but paused when he recognized Rol. He was Gilgamesh's cousin and only son of his uncle Croft. Rol and Gilgamesh were raised like siblings in the court of the dark elves—Gilgamesh the rightful heir to the throne of the black forest, and Rol the resentful little prince who always felt cheated out of his chance to lead. Rol was a privileged little asshole, known for his abrasive personality and smug grin, but that night, he wasn't grinning. His eyes were frightened as if he had looked into the very pits of hell and knew what awaited them all on the other side.

"My cousin . . . where is my cousin?" Rol staggered through the crowd, barely able to keep his footing.

"I am here, Rol." Gilgamesh stepped forward. It was then

that he noticed the black blood staining Rol's shirt. "Cousin, what has happened?"

"Betrayed us . . . Titus has betrayed us all . . . the end of days are upon us," Rol rambled. His legs weakened and he almost collapsed, but Gilgamesh caught him and held him upright. Rol was feverish and his dark skin ashen.

Gilgamesh felt that sickness in the pit of his gut again. Rol was looking like he was going to pass out, so he grabbed him by his shoulders and shook him to keep him lucid until he got the answers he needed. "Cousin, where is Croft? Where is my uncle?"

"Dead," Rol sobbed. "My father is dead, as we all will be soon." Rol began fading again, but Gilgamesh shook him. Rol stood up straight and mumbled something in elvish that Gilgamesh only caught pieces of. Rol clasped Gilgamesh's face in his hands and looked him in the eyes. For a minute, Rol appeared coherent again. "I know the secret of the betrayer, cousin. He has made fools of us all. The end of days is upon us, and we are powerless to stop what is to come." He gasped before falling into Gilgamesh's arms and going still.

Asha and the others watched in saddened silence as Gilgamesh cradled his cousin to him lovingly. When Rol's life-force fled his body, it became a little more than an empty husk of skin and magic. Gilgamesh ran his hands through his cousin's hair, and the strands began to fall away like dry twigs. He hugged Rol's frame to him, and the body began to crumble. The wind came along and swept away what was left of Rol, like dead leaves blowing down a New York street. For a long while Gilgamesh just stood there, pieces of his cousin still clinging to his suit.

"Mesh . . ." Teko took a step toward him, but Gilgamesh waved him away.

Gilgamesh closed his eyes and took several calming breaths. When he opened his eyes again, they burned like two purple suns. His voice was calm when he spoke, but there was no mistaking the weight of his words. "Now, it's personal."

· CHAPTER THREE ·

John Rogue was coasting on what could only be described as the mother of all drugs, if it could actually be purchased in a pharmacy or on a street corner. His body twisted on waves of bliss that threatened to pull him under, but the nagging sensation that he was leaving something undone kept him from giving in to the sweet nothing. He was in the thrall of the shadows.

Rogue was born human . . . slightly more than human if you counted the fact that he was also born a mage, descended from a powerful line of death magic practitioners. He was a competent enough spell caster, but had never really tapped into his powers until his father and little brother had called on him to help banish a shadow demon back to the pit. His brother had been trying to conjure a spirit but pulled the demon across by accident and lost control of him. The demon had become fascinated with humanity and had no intention of returning to the shadow pit. He was too powerful a demon to be simply cast back, so they bargained with him. In exchange for him not unleashing his wrath on humanity and crawling back into the pit, he and Rogue would swap eyes so he could still experience the simple joys of the mortal world. The bargain allowed the demon to experience the world as Rogue did, when Rogue allowed him, but it also allowed the young mage to tap into the power of shadows. This made Rogue a powerful spell caster, but it came with a price. The more he tapped into the shadows, the greater the risk of him being sucked into the collective. With the shadows, there was no individuality, only one collective intellect.

There was a ripple in the shadow tide that jarred Rogue. Groggily, he came out of his drift, his mind trying to fight through the haze. The pull of the shadows was so seductive that his body wanted to be lost in it forever, but his mind clung to reality. There was another ripple, this one stronger and more defined so it pierced the darkness, and he was able to make out what it was—screaming. The chilling sound snapped him out of it, and he remembered his mission and the urgency of it.

Jackson, one of the young misfits who had taken up their quest to stop Titus, was down on one knee. The knuckles of one of his armored fists were buried into the ground, trying to help him keep his balance, while his other hand tried frantically to keep his intestines from spilling out onto the dirt floor of the scrap yard. Hovering over him was a man, if you could still call him that. With large black wings, edged with razor sharp feathers, and wielding a scythe, the creature looked more like a dark angel. Rogue wasn't sure what it was or who had sent it, but it stank of death magic. The death angel raised one of its razor-edged wings to finish Jackson off, and moving more from will than conscious actions, Rogue lashed out with the shadows.

The dark angel's wing slashed through the air, on course for Jackson's exposed neck, when it was ensnared by shadows. It raised the hand holding the scythe to free itself, and more shadows attacked, latching onto its arms and legs. The angel raged, pulling at the shadows, and Rogue slowly emerged from the concrete, like a slow bubbling black spring, solidifying as they struggled. His long dreads had long ago come loose from the leather band that held them in a neat ponytail and crowned his face like a lion's mane. The power of shadow magic made Rogue stronger than most, but the angel was stronger. It yanked forward, causing Rogue to stumble, and dislodging his sunglasses from his brown face and exposing his eyes. To most outsiders, Rogue passed for human, but his eyes gave away his secret and the price he had paid to the shadow demon. They were dark pools of black flaked with starlight. Looking into them was like looking up at a Nebraska sky on a crisp autumn night.

The angel threw its wings wide and shredded the shadows that held it. It moved in on Rogue with incredible speed, but he still had time to clear one of the two revolvers he carried. One was loaded with regular hollow point bullets and the other with special enchanted bullets, which were especially effective against the supernatural. Rogue squeezed the trigger of the mystic gun just as the angel attacked with one of its wings, striking the gun and sending the shot wild. Before he could get off another one, the angel knocked the gun from his hand and grabbed Rogue by his throat.

Rogue delivered two blows to the angel's ribs that would've broken the bones of a mortal, but the angel was unfazed. The angel had a firm grip on Rogue's neck and was trying his best to snap it. As they continued to struggle, Rogue got a good look at the angel for the first time and found its features familiar. Its stringy white hair, pale blue eyes . . . Rogue knew that face.

"Brother Julius?" Rogue croaked.

"Don't speak that name!" The angel darted at Rogue, swinging its scythe wildly. Brother Julius had been second-in-command to High Brother Angelo and captain of the Inquisition, the honor guard who protected the house of Sanctuary and sometimes enforced its decrees. Sanctuary had been a refuge for men and demons, as well as one of the greatest sources of information on the supernatural world and the things that dwelled in it. For nearly a millennium, the great house had stood tall and proud, but now it lay in ruin on a forgotten block in Manhattan. The great house and most that dwelled in it had been destroyed, including Brother Julius. They had all seen him fall under the goblin blade, but someone or something had brought him back from the Dead Lands as an abomination of the two worlds. Rogue knew there was only one creature who could perform such a trick.

Rogue tried to reason with him. "Brother Julius, listen to me. Whatever Ezrah has done to you can be undone."

Brother Julius clasped his hands over his ears, shaking his head violently as if the words pained him. "Lies . . . more lies. The world is filled with lies and the only truth is in death."

"Please, let us help you." Finnious crept forward. He was a pale youth with lovely black curls and black eyes. Being the product of a nymph who was raped by the King of the Dead Lands, he too was an abomination of two worlds, but found a home at Sanctuary. He had been with High Brother Angelo during his last feverish moments. With his dying breath, he had placed something inside Fin and told him it was the last piece of magic that remained of the great house. Finnious didn't ask for the gift, but now that he had it, there was a very healthy price tag hanging from his head.

Julius turned to Fin and covered his eyes against the light radiating from him that very few could see. "The Spark." His voice was shaky. "Give it!" He launched at Finnious.

Finnious was too terrified to move, so he just stood there with his eyes clamped shut, trembling. There was a gust of wind, and he prepared himself for the death strike, but it never came. When he opened his eyes, the death angel was stumbling forward, a few feet past him. When Finnious examined himself, he realized his body was almost transparent. He had phased out again. Normally he would've been upset with himself about the lack of self-control, but this time he was thankful for it.

Julius let out a screech that sounded more animal than human and charged again. Rogue tried to erect a web of shadow to slow him down, but Julius tore through it like tissue paper, eyes locked on Finnious. He raised his scythe, glowing ghostly white, infused with the power of the Dead Lands, and struck. The howling of tortured souls trapped in the hereafter could be heard as the blade cut through the air. This time, he wouldn't be denied . . . or so he thought.

There was a flash of gold, followed by the sounds of steel on steel. The scythe spun end over end and lost itself in a pile of scrap metal a few yards away. Julius snarled and turned his accusing blue eyes on the one who dared stand between him and his task. She was a petite Asian girl with a cute face and long, black hair. Her useless eyes were shut tight, instead sensing the world through her ears as she'd been forced to do since birth. Clutched in her hand was a golden spear with two pointed edges. Like Morgan's hammer, the Spear of Truth was one of the anointed weapons that had been used by the Knights of Christ during the Siege.

Her name was Lydia Osheda, descendant of Sinjin Osheda, a wizard and weapons master who was said to have crafted the very weapon she recently discovered had been hiding in her walking stick for years. Though she was born blind, she was hardly defenseless. Lydia worked ten times as hard as the other initiates at Sanctuary to hone her skills. She was barely out of her teens but could wield sword or spear better than some who had been studying twice as long. She was another of the displaced refugees of Sanctuary who had been sucked into the battle between good and evil raging in New York City.

"Brother Julius, I know there is still the good man we all knew hiding somewhere in there. Do not let it take the spilling of more blood to bring him out," Lydia said. High Brother Angelo had been her guardian, but it was Brother Julius whom she had practiced with for hours on end honing her sword skills. Using what he'd taught her against him was not something she looked forward to.

"I will have the Spark!" Julius snarled.

"Then you'll go through me to get it." Lydia raised the spear and took a defensive stance. Her ears picked up the rush of air when Julius drew his wings back, and she moved accordingly, spinning with the breeze when the first wave of dagger-like feathers whistled past. In a fluid motion, she brought the spear around and went for one of his eyes, but Julius caught the spear midstrike. They danced around in a semicircle, each trying to wrest the spear from the other.

"Out of the way, kid, I've got him," Rogue said. He had

retrieved his enchanted gun and was trying to get a clear shot at Julius.

"No!" she yelled, continuing to struggle. "I have to at least try, Rogue." Julius reached for her hair, but she ducked away, turning the spear counterclockwise, splitting it in half. Julius still held one, but with the other, she slashed him across his chest, only deep enough to draw blood and get his attention. She still believed that she could reason with him. "Julius, please, let us help you!"

Julius clawed at his hair, pulling it out in white clumps. He was confused, torn between the magic Ezrah had worked on him and what he felt in his heart. "I can't . . . I will . . . the Spark." He staggered back and forth. "I must!" With a flap of his wings, he was airborne and streaking toward Lydia and Fin, resolved to cut her down to get to the Spark.

The man Lydia had known as Brother Julius was gone, and with a heavy heart, she had to accept it and do what was necessary. Lydia dropped back like she was in a limbo contest, narrowly missing the dark wings that tried to claim her head. As he passed over, she sliced through his wings, knocking him off course and sending him spilling to the ground. Julius, on his hands and knees, watched as Lydia approached him. "I'm sorry it had to end this way." She drove both halves of the spear into his hand, pinning him to the ground. "Now, Rogue!" she shouted.

Rogue appeared from the shadows, enchanted gun in hand. The bullets from that gun were bespelled with death magic far older than some species and said to be able to kill anything that was of the supernatural. Rogue placed the gun to the side of Julius's head. "I'll make it clean," he said to Lydia before pulling the trigger.

The bullet spat from the gun as little more than a sliver of light. It rattled around in Julius's head, pouring light from his eyes and mouth like a jack-o-lantern. When the light faded, a peaceful expression crossed Julius's face. He looked from Rogue then to Lydia. He reached up to touch the leg of her jeans, but his hand disintegrated and blew away on the wind. His body soon followed, leaving nothing of Brother Julius other than a stain and memories.

Lydia dropped to her knees in the spot where Julius had fallen. She ran her hands back and forth over the earth and said a silent prayer for the fallen brother. Her heart was heavy, but she was unable to cry, so she wept inside. High Brother Angelo and Brother Julius had been like her surrogate parents and Sanctuary had been her home. Now, they were all gone. Fin walked up beside Lydia, placing his hand on her shoulder and giving it a gentle squeeze. She placed her hand over his and stroked it. They were all that remained of the place that had provided refuge for so many.

Rogue came to stand beside them. He was wiping his sunglasses off on his shirt. "You kids okay?"

Finnious nodded, but Lydia remained silent.

Rogue's heart went out to them. They were just kids and had been through more in the past few days than some adults would go through in a lifetime. He decided to allow them their space to grieve and went to check on Jonas and Jackson.

Jonas knelt over his fallen comrade, speaking softly to him. He must've sensed Rogue's presence because he spared a glance over his shoulder. His hood was pulled over his head, shadowing his pale green face, but Rogue could see the fabric wriggling with movement from the half-dozen snakes that crowned his head. He was the last of his kind, the Medusan, a race of ancient beings who watched and recorded events of the world since the dawn of man.

Rogue looked down at Jackson, who was lying on his back in a pool of his own blood. His belly was splayed open like a pig in a slaughter house, and he bled freely onto the ground. Jackson's skin looked ashen, and his eyes were glassy as if he couldn't focus. When he noticed Rogue, he gave him a weak smile.

"How bad is it?" Jackson asked.

Rogue smiled. "It's just a scratch. You're gonna be fine," he lied. He could see Jackson's intestines sticking out of his wound. It was a wonder he had even lasted this long.

"Man, I'm glad you're a better shot than you are a liar." Jackson tried to laugh, but broke into a fit of coughing, sending blood spilling down the sides of his face. "Damn, this hurts."

"Jackson, just lie still. I'm going to patch you up like I always do," Jonas assured him.

Jackson shook his head weakly. "Jonas, I think this is a little more severe than a broken bone or a few stitches. I'm going to the Upper Room. Tell Red I'm sorry I kicked the bucket before I paid him back."

"You can tell him yourself. You're not going to die, so stop talking like it," Jonas snapped. He hadn't meant to, but he was becoming emotional. In his centuries of aimless wandering of the earth, he had always avoided making attachments with humans. It wasn't until he met Morgan and Jackson, and they formed their little family, did he open up. They were all he had. "Rogue, maybe you can bandage the wound with shadow magic?" he asked desperately.

"Jonas, even if I could wrap the wound, I can't close it. It's too deep. I'm sorry," Rogue said sadly.

"Let me try." Finnious stepped forward.

"Finnious, you want to try this again after what happened with Angelo?" Rogue asked. The day before, he had tried to save the life of High Brother Angelo, and not only failed but almost died in the process.

Finnious nodded. "If there's a chance, then I have to at least try. Please, let me try."

Rogue and Jonas exchanged suspicious glances. Jonas was hesitant, but he moved to the side to allow Finnious room to kneel over Jackson.

Jackson gave a weak laugh. "How ironic is this—a wraith who's trying to save a life instead of taking it. I wish Red were here to see this."

"*Half*-wraith," Finnious corrected him. He raised his hands and looked at them with uncertainty. "This is not going to be painless." Jackson nodded that he understood. Finnious took a deep breath and plunged his hands into Jackson's wound.

Jackson howled in pain as Fin worked his fingers through muscle and intestines, exploring the cut. A low white light began to pulse from Fin's body as his form wavered between the here and there while he worked. In his mind, he saw the inside of Jackson's body, damaged nerves and severed muscles, and concentrated on them first, stitching and reconnecting the tissue. It was a slow and tedious process, but Finnious stayed focused. Partially through his repairs, he felt a force coming from Jackson brush against his consciousness that made him take a good look at Jackson. He didn't notice it at first, but when he used his ghost sight, he was able to see it. Something dark clung to Jackson's soul like a second skin. Fin tried to make contact with whatever it was and was thrown back violently.

"Are you okay, Fin?" Rogue helped him to his feet.

"Something . . . I don't know . . ." Finnious tried to get the words out, but was too rattled to speak.

"By the gods, it worked!" Jonas exclaimed.

They rushed over, with a visibly shaken Finnious bringing up the rear. He was almost too afraid to look at Jackson, but when he did, he gasped. The wound was all but healed, save for a bloody cut that ran across his stomach.

"I owe you quite the debt for saving him. Thank you, Finnious." Jonas embraced him.

Fin just nodded and grinned. He should've been relieved that Jackson would live, but he wasn't. He knew that his magic had repaired some of the damage, but he had not the time or the skill to take credit for what he was seeing. Again calling his ghost sight, he examined Jackson. He could no longer see the malevolent force, but he could still feel it lurking beneath the surface.

"If he's whole enough to move, then we should get him inside. We're sitting ducks if something else jumps out of the woodwork," Rogue pointed out.

No sooner had Rogue said it, than the wind seemed to pick up out of nowhere, sending trash and debris flying through the scrap yard. Between them and the entrance of Jonas's lair, the very fabric of reality seemed to split open like a zipper, and they could see silhouettes moving toward them from within. Rogue stood at the ready with his two revolvers, with Lydia flanking him and Jonas huddled over Jackson protectively.

"Whatever comes through that rift, kill it and ask questions later!" Rogue shouted to Lydia over the howling wind.

Lydia nodded, tightening her grip on the Spear of Truth.

A figure stepped from the tear, armed with a blade that

glowed with the same color as the energy that spilled from the portal. Rogue was about to open fire, but he realized he had seen the swordsman before, only a few hours prior. He touched Lydia's arm to let her know to stand down and moved to meet the man.

"Nice trick. Do you do weddings too?" Rogue asked the Gammurai. Teko ignored him, instead looking past him at the scene and the new faces. When he had deemed they were no threat, he looked over his shoulder at the tear and nodded to whatever or whoever was on the other side.

Gilgamesh stepped through next. Gone was his suit, and he wore only black pants and a black shirt under a midnight cloak. His eyes were hard and angry. Seeing Gilgamesh was unexpected, but even more of a shock was that he had Morgan and Asha with him.

"Jackson?" Morgan called out, noticing his best friend splayed on the ground. He bull-charged through the startled onlookers and rushed to where Jonas knelt over Jackson. "What's happened? Who has done this?" He was furious and wanted someone to turn his anger on.

Jonas placed a calming hand on his shoulder. "Jackson will live, thank the gods. I'll tell you of the things that passed, but another has already settled the score." He nodded at Rogue.

Morgan looked over, then turned back to Jackson. He nodded in understanding. "Then it's yet another debt I'll owe to the mage."

"We all owe John Rogue, but we can take a tally of favors after we get Jackson inside," Jonas told him.

Morgan scooped Jackson in his arms like a child and carried him back inside the compound. Jonas lingered for a few seconds then followed him.

Rogue's eyes were on Asha. She looked worn out, and blood stained her clothes . . . again. When she looked up at him, the sadness in her eyes hit him like a physical blow. Without even thinking about it, he went to her and pulled her into a tight hug.

"Are you hurt?" Rogue held her at arm's length and examined her. Seeing the condition she was in angered him, and he flashed a not-so-friendly look at Gilgamesh. "What the hell happened?"

"It's not my blood." Asha shoved him away. Her rejection stung, but Rogue didn't show it.

Rogue turned to his childhood friend. "Mesh, what is this all about?"

"The witch's story isn't mine to tell. As far as my presence here, you wanted the help of the dark elves and now you have it," Gilgamesh said.

"Bullshit, and you know it. When I came to you a few hours ago, you were adamant about not getting involved because there was nothing to gain, and now you're all in? Don't play me. What happened to business and never personal?" Rogue asked.

"It became personal when I held my cousin in my arms and watched his soul called back to the darkness," Gilgamesh said.

"Rol?" Rogue had known Mesh's cousin from their days as kids. He and Rol had never gotten along, but he was still family by extension. "I'm sorry, Mesh. Does Croft know yet?"

"He's dead too. Titus cut the fingers from the Black Hand, but the knuckles of that hand live on." Gilgamesh pounded his chest fiercely. "Now that you know my reasons, let's get to the business of revenge. You're entrenched in this, John, so I will assume that you have a plan?"

"Yeah, get in and out of the Iron Mountains without getting killed," Rogue said seriously.

"A sound plan, but why would we go to the Iron Mountains when Titus is at Raven Wood?" Gilgamesh asked.

"Because like I told you earlier, I've got some friends stuck down in that shit hole, and I intend to bring them out," Rogue replied.

Gilgamesh shook his head. "John, what do you think the chances are that your humans are even still alive? Why risk it possibly for nothing?"

"Because friends don't leave friends for dead when they need help." Rogue didn't mask the venom in his voice when he spoke. "If they're dead, then I need to see a body before I just write them off."

Gilgamesh wasn't pleased with the detour, but he understood. "Fine, John. We'll go to the Iron Mountains, but the moment we have proof that your friends are either alive or dead, we leave for Raven Wood. We're in and we're out. No more detours."

Rogue nodded. "Fair enough, Mesh."

"I'm going too," Lydia spoke up.

"Not this time, kid. We're going into the goblins' stronghold, and it's gonna get real nasty, real quick. I don't want to risk something happening to you while we're down there," Rogue said.

Lydia raised the Spear of Truth, which was still stained with Julius's blood. "Have I not proven that I can take care of myself?"

"Yeah, you're good, kid, but good doesn't guarantee your survival under the mountains," Rogue said seriously. "We're keeping our numbers small so we have a better chance of getting in and out undetected."

"But, Rogue . . ."

"No arguments," he said, cutting her off. "Lydia." He placed his hand on her shoulder. "I know what they took from you, so I understand your need for revenge, but this is bigger than personal grudges. Mankind is at stake in this. If we go down there and don't make it out, you and the others will be the last line of defense and the only things standing between Titus and the rest of the free world. Do you understand?"

Lydia nodded. "Yes, Rogue."

Finnious took Lydia's hand. "C'mon, let's see if we can help with Jackson." He pulled her toward the bunker. Reluctantly, she went with him.

Asha came to stand beside Rogue. He acknowledged her presence with a glance, but kept his focus on Lydia and Fin until they had disappeared through the garage and onto the elevator to the lower levels of the bunker. "You've got to admire and pity those two," he began. "They've had the foundation of their lives ripped away in the fight and are still willing to fight."

"Sometimes the fight is all you have left to hold onto," Asha said.

"Is that what keeps you going?" he asked.

Asha thought on it for a few seconds. "I guess," she said with a shrug. "Maybe when I come back, I'll know the answer to that question."

"Like I told Lydia, we cannot all go rumbling into the Iron Mountains," Rogue said.

Asha laughed. "I'll leave the suicide missions to you guys. I've got something I need to take care of in Manhattan."

"That'll be damn near as dangerous as going into the Iron Mountains with Titus and all his minions looking for us, or have you forgotten we're all at the top of his shit list?" Rogue reminded her.

Asha looked down at her bloody clothes. "No, I was reminded of that when the man I trusted above all others sent my best friends to kill me."

This surprised Rogue. "Why would Dutch try to have you killed when you're so close to finding out what's going on?"

"Maybe I'm too close," Asha suggested. "I don't know, but I intend to find out."

"So you think you're just gonna march into the Triple Six and demand that he come clean?" Rogue asked sarcastically.

"No, I'm gonna ask nicely first. If that doesn't work"—she slipped her bladed rings over her thumbs—"I'll ask not so nicely."

Rogue shook his head. "You know you're asking for trouble, don't you?"

"Of course I do, but it is what it is. I need answers, and Dutch is going to give them to me."

"You be careful, little blood witch," Rogue said.

"Don't worry about me, Rogue. You aren't the only one who's good at moving undetected." Asha whispered a spell and vanished into the night.

"She's good," Gilgamesh said. Rogue hadn't even noticed him standing there.

"Yeah, she is. So, you ready to go?"

"We were waiting on you."

"How far to the nearest rip?" Rogue asked. A rip was a tear in the fabric of reality between the mortal realm and the kingdoms of Midland. The rips were becoming fewer and fewer as the age of technology more gradually forced magic out.

"Closer than you think." Gilgamesh nodded at Teko.

"You mean to tell me you've had the rip standing next to

you the whole time and made me jump through hoops?"
Rogue was angry, thinking about how he'd come to Gilgamesh
for help finding a rip to get them to the Iron Mountains, and
his friend had given him the runaround.

"Not me, the blade." Teko held the sword up for Rogue to
examine.

Rogue looked at the blade closely. Through his shadow
eyes, the veils of the mortal world fell away, and he could see
the blade for what it *really* was. It was an elvish blade in design, but not the enchantment that empowered it. He could
not identify the magical signature resonating from it, but he
knew it was old and powerful magic. In all his travels, he had
never heard of a weapon that could tear through the veils of
realms, but apparently the dark elves had a few tricks up their
sleeves that they weren't sharing with everyone else. He couldn't
say he was surprised. The dark elves had always been among
the more secretive of the supernatural races. He stored the information in his head, in case he needed to use it later as
either a bargaining chip or insurance.

"Teko can open a rip that will get us close to the goblin
stronghold, but we'll be flying blind from there to find your
friends," Gilgamesh said.

"Then we best get moving." Rogue checked his guns.

"So, are we to cover all that ground on foot?" Gilgamesh
asked.

"Unless you have a better idea, yes."

"I have a suggestion." Teko looked over at the Hummer
they had appropriated from Sanctuary.

· CHAPTER FOUR ·

Raven Wood was quiet, quieter than it had been in the past few nights. The expansive estate was owned by prominent fashion designer Mario Bucaddo, but in name only. It was really the New York haven of Maxwell Titus. To the world at large, Max Titus was a forty-something billionaire who owned and operated a major corporation north of the Canadian border, Titus Corp. He spent most of his time hidden away in his glass tower in downtown Ontario, only leaving under extreme circumstances such as the ones that had brought him to New York. Titus was a very secretive man and with good reason. There was no telling how some of his business partners would feel knowing that they were doing business with a halfling.

Titus was a man trapped between two worlds, those of men and demons. At one time he had been a Knight of Christ and servant of the church, but his lust for power outweighed his faith. While his brothers at arms drew and shed blood on the battlefield, Titus was in the shadows bargaining with the dark lord. In exchange for bringing them the Nimrod, Titus would reign as a god on earth. When Titus made his play to betray the Bishop for the Nimrod, the magic rebelled against him and almost cost him his life. When Titus was struck down with the very weapon he'd stolen, one of the points broke off in his chest and to that day remained lodged in his heart. The magic from the shard buried within him was the reason why he aged far slower than an average human, but it was also the thing that kept him from being made a full demon, as was his heart's desire.

The deity Titus served, a demon called Belthon, had been the guiding hand behind the original Seven Day Siege and the force orchestrating the events leading up to that day. In exchange for Titus betraying his holy order and pledging himself to Belthon, he would be granted a seat at the big boy table when the end of days came about. To remove the shard would likely mean his death, so instead, Belthon used Titus as a conduit between here and there to try and bring about hell on earth through more conventional means.

In his service to the dark lord, Titus had become the favorite, hatching countless plots and adding to the power of the dark forces, but always falling short of their ultimate goal to conquer humanity. When the Trident of Heaven resurfaced, he saw an opportunity to finish what he had started four centuries prior and reopen the Dark Storm, but once again, a Redfeather stood between him and glory. He'd thought wresting the Nimrod from the awkward young man would be a simple thing, but it was proving to be quite the opposite. The longer Gabriel remained in possession of the trident, the stronger the bond between them became, and the harder it would be to part them. Time was not on Titus's side.

With thoughts of conquest and murder running through his head, Titus enjoyed the show being put on for him in the middle of the floor. There were two naked women, one a blonde and one a brunette, making love to each other. The blonde was called Helena, she was Titus's attendant. The brunette was an escort they'd had brought in for entertainment and other purposes.

The girl's head lolled back while Helena suckled at her neck. She felt like she was floating on a wave of pure bliss and slipping further away by the second. The escort's body went limp, while Helena cradled her in her arms and continued sucking at her neck. Only when the escort's heart had stopped beating did the vampire Helena tear herself away.

She threw her head back as if she was gasping for air and let out a giddy laugh. Her tight golden curls fell away from her face, allowing the light from the fireplace to play tricks on her pale skin. Blood dripped from her lips to the corpse beneath her, staining the nipple. Helena dipped her head and lapped the blood from the nipple like a cat, looking up at Titus seductively. Titus sat on the couch, rubbing his hand across his crotch absently. He was half demon, but also half mortal and still enjoyed mortal pleasures. With his free hand, he beckoned Helena to come to him.

On all fours, Helena crawled toward Titus. When she reached him, she sat up on her knees so he could admire her firm breasts. Helena was 118 years old, but had been fortunate enough to be made a vampire at a young age, so she would be forever beautiful. She took one of Titus's hands and placed it over her breast. He played with the erect nipple using only his index finger and thumb. The fresh blood Helena had ingested was like a hit from a designer drug, so his touch sent vibrations through her body.

Titus grabbed her by the back of her neck and pulled her onto his lap. He kissed her deeply, tasting the blood of the escort she'd just fed on. Helena reached between her legs until she found what she was looking for and pulled his erect penis from the loose silk pants he wore. She mounted him slowly, breathing the sweet smell of fresh death into his face. Helena rode Titus's lap, whispering sweetly into his ear. She had been around the favorite son long enough to know what it took to stroke his ego, and the fact that she knew spoke for why she had outlasted the others.

Still inside her, Titus turned her around and began thrusting in and out of her while she bounced on his lap. Helena's nails tore deep gouges in the arms of the wooden chair. Titus positioned himself so that he was behind her now. He grabbed a handful of her curls and began to pump deeply.

While Titus punished Helena, darkness blanked the window behind him, shutting out the moonlight. The inky blackness oozed from the window and pooled in the middle of the floor, taking the shape of a man. Moses the Shadow Master stood in the center of the room, silently watching Titus and Helena curiously. The shadow demon no longer felt urges like love or lust, but he would occasionally enjoy a woman when he took a human host.

Helena looked over her shoulder at the shadow master and asked, "Are you going to stand there gawking or join us?"

Moses cast his eyes to the ground. "I would have a word in private with our lord Titus."

"Your words can wait, shadow. Can't you see that our lord

is occupied?" Helena pressed herself into Titus, urging him to go deeper.

"It's about the Rising," Moses said.

Titus stopped his throttling of Helena. He leaned in and whispered to her, "Clean up your mess and leave us. We'll continue this later." He removed himself from her and gave her a playful slap on the ass.

Helena mumbled something under her breath and went to do as she was told. As she strode nude past Moses, she bared her fangs and hissed at him. She grabbed the corpse by its hair and dragged it from the room to give Titus and Moses their privacy.

Titus addressed Moses. "For you to interrupt my little romp, I'll assume what you have to say is of importance?"

"Indeed, my lord. Riel and I have retrieved the blood and delivered it to the warlock."

"That's excellent news. Soon we will be able to commence the Rising and usher in the new age. From your mood when you came, I'd expected to be disturbed by whatever news you'd brought," Titus said.

"I also bring news of treachery among our ranks." Moses seemed to ooze when he moved to stand closer to Titus so they might whisper, as if some unseen enemy would hear their exchange. "Something passed through the veil from the Dead Lands and attacked the champions, but not to reclaim the Nimrod for the dark order. I think he was after the Spark that is said to be carried within the wraith." He'd expected Titus to be upset to hear of the Ezrah's true motives, but surprisingly he wasn't.

Titus shrugged. "Then he's welcome to burn in the pursuit of it . . . again. For as powerful as the Spark is, it'll be little more than a flashlight in the darkness once I am in possession of the Nimrod and complete the Rising. His preoccupation is actually a boon to us. While he's chasing the Spark, he's none the wiser of the souls we've been plucking from the Dead Lands for the Rising. The twelve shall walk and our enemies shall fall. Now, if that's all, I have preparations to make." Titus turned to leave.

"I have one last bit of information," Moses informed him. He waited until Titus beckoned for him to continue before speaking again. "One of the Valkrin escorts has gone rogue."

Titus's eyes flashed anger. "What do you mean, *has gone rogue?*"

"She went with a troop of goblins to investigate a disturbance in the tunnels and none of them returned. They say she now fights on the side of the light."

"Why in the nine hells was one of my personal bodyguards sent to do footwork for goblins?" Titus raged. He grabbed a glass from the table and hurled it at Moses's head, but it passed right through the shadow.

"The demon was in Riel's charge, not mine," Moses reminded him.

Titus shook his head sadly. "I'm surrounded by idiots and turncoats."

"The shadows will be forever loyal," Moses assured him.

"Of this I am sure, my old friend, which is why you still serve me. What was the name of the traitor?" Titus asked.

"The one called Mercy," Moses informed him.

"I should've known the bond between mother and daughter would be stronger than the call of battle. No matter, she and her offspring will be punished accordingly. Where is the traitor now?"

Moses closed his eyes and communicated with the collective of shadows. When he opened them, he looked worried.

"She is on the threshold of the Iron Mountains with the young half-breed girl and the boy."

Titus's head snapped up. "The Nimrod is in Midland?"

"Yes, my lord."

Titus's blood ran cold. Though he and the goblins were allies, the thought of one of them capturing the Nimrod didn't sit well with him. Then a much more frightening thought crept into his mind. He had hidden the sprite Leah away in the Iron Mountains because he wanted to keep her as far away from magic as possible, and the equivalent of a mystic nuclear bomb was about to be within arm's reach.

"Pull Orden from whatever whore he's ravaging and tell him to make ready for travel. I'll have Flagg prepare a portal, but he and Riel will stay behind. You're with me," Titus told him.

"Where are we going, my lord?" Moses asked.

"We're going to the Iron Mountains. I've heard quite a bit about this Gabriel Redfeather. It is time I look upon him with my own eyes, before I rip the Nimrod from his corpse."

• CHAPTER FIVE •

When Gabriel got his first look at the Iron Mountains, he couldn't help but gawk in amazement. They were still several miles away from the actual mountains, but he could see them in the distance. The goblin stronghold was a monstrous structure that was carved into the base of the mountain itself. Rivers of lava flowed from openings in the mountains into the valley. From the intense heat it was no wonder hardly anything grew within the mountain. Few plants could flourish under those conditions.

"Welcome to hell." Mercy stood beside him.

"Sounds about right to me." DeMona joined them. "So that's the goblin stronghold?"

"Stolen from its rightful owners, the dwarves," Cristobel added.

"Hopefully before it's all said and done, we can steal it back for you guys," DeMona told him.

"Quiet." Gilchrist stumbled forward. His gnarled ears perked up as if he was listening for something.

"What's wrong?" Gabriel asked him.

"Hear it, you cannot?" Gilchrist put his ear to the ground.

Gabriel couldn't hear anything, but he could tell by the looks on DeMona's and Mercy's faces that they too could hear whatever it was that troubled the goblin. "Sounds like marching, coming from over that hill!" Mercy pointed to a dune a few yards away.

"I'll check it out," Gabriel volunteered. He started forward, but Mercy stopped him.

She crept forward. "And risk you giving away our position with your lumbering? I don't think so." She crawled on her belly to the edge of the dune looking over the valley. Just below were a dozen goblins marching through. Trailing not far behind them were two wagons being pulled by what looked like oversized ferrets. On one wagon was a cage carrying slaves, and on the other was a box covered by a black tarp. The goblin who led them looked less like a goblin than most as he was spared the deformities that were so common among their species. He had smooth yellow skin with stringy purple hair that hung to his knees. He could almost pass for human had it not been for his reptilian eyes. He was Orden's second-in-command.

"What do you think is under the tarp?" DeMona whispered, startling her mother.

"Old magic," Mercy said simply. She was impressed that DeMona was able to sneak up on her undetected. There may have been hope for her yet.

"Holy shit!" DeMona blurted out.

"What is it?" Mercy asked.

"Look in the cage."

Mercy let her eyes roam over the faces in the cage until she picked out the familiar one. It was the old man, Gabriel's grandfather. He didn't look well at all, and one of his arms was heavily bandaged with a bloodstained cloth. There was also a girl who Mercy had never seen, with her head resting on his lap. She looked sick and didn't seem to be conscious. A young dwarf woman with flowing red hair dabbed a cloth along the girl's forehead. Her touch was caring, but her eyes looked doubtful.

"I guess we won't have to go into the mountain after all, since they've brought our friends to us." DeMona stood to make her way down the hill and engage the goblins.

Mercy quickly snatched her back. "Not like that. There are too many of them, and we'll be butchered before we even reach the wagons."

"They can't kill us if they don't see us coming." Gabriel stood. He raised the trident to the heavens and forced his will into it. There was the crack of thunder in the distance, followed by a dense fog that rolled over the hill and down into the valley.

Redfeather felt delirious. He had heard stories about the horrors that went on under the Iron Mountains, but the stories failed to do them justice. The goblins had truly given him a glimpse into hell and made sure he was reminded of it every time he looked down at the bloody stump where his hand used to be.

The goblins had done their worst, breaking his body, but his spirit held fast. He held on to the faint sliver of hope that Lucy would escape and get word back to his grandson of what fate had befallen him, but that hope died when her body was brought back to the stronghold. There was no sign of the dwarf Cristobel, and Lucy hadn't been able to speak to tell if he was alive or dead. She had succumbed to some sort of poison and was in a coma. The young dwarf woman Mavis, who she had come in with, was somewhat of a healer, but she had not the skill or the necessary tools to do much for Lucy besides try to keep her comfortable. It was doubtful that she would last through the night without the proper attention, and the goblins were less than accommodating in that right.

Redfeather felt the wagon stop suddenly. He peered through the bars and noticed a heavy fog rolling into the valley, making it difficult to see. There was a scream, followed by the sounds of battle. What he heard next restored hope in his heart.

"Grandfather!"

When Illini noticed the fog, he raised his hand for the caravan to halt. He drew his long staff and strained his eyes to see through the mist.

"Witchcraft?" the goblin warrior standing closest to him asked.

Illini's brow furred. "No, we've got visitors." He turned to the goblin steering the wagon that carried the cube. "Continue on to the tower and under no circumstances are you to stop. If you even slow down, I'll cut off your head and drink wine from your skull, do you understand?" The goblin nodded and Illini slapped him. "Then why are you still here? Move!" The goblin on the wagon cracked the reins and pressed the mutant ferret forward. "The rest of you," he addressed his troop, "prepare for battle."

No sooner had the words left his mouth, than something leapt from the fog. It was a human who he did not know, but he recognized the weapon he carried. It was the Trident of Heaven.

Gabriel moved far more gracefully than he previously had, weaving and striking between the goblins. An anxious monster leapt from the throng with designs on taking Gabriel's head with his short sword. For his effort, he was rewarded by finding himself impaled on the points of the Nimrod. Gabriel placed his hand on the goblin's head, and his body lit up like a Christmas tree before crumbling to dust. From the darkness burst the wagon that was carrying the caged slaves. The driver tried to run Gabriel down, but Gabriel leapt high in the air and brought the trident around, stabbing him through the throat. With a sharp twist, he relieved the goblin of his head.

"Grandfather!" Gabriel rushed around to the side of the cage.

The elder Redfeather clutched a bar with one hand and shed tears of joy at the sight of his grandson. "Thank God, you're alive. For as thrilled as I am to see you, coming here was not wise, Gabriel."

"I couldn't just leave you, Granddad. Are you hurt?" Gabriel asked, looking over his badly bruised grandfather. When his eyes landed on the bloody stump, he almost broke down in tears. "What have they done to you?"

"I'll live, thank God," Redfeather said. "How did you find me?"

"I can fill you in later. Right now, I need to find a way to get you out of this cage." Gabriel began searching the cage for a door.

"Behind you!" Redfeather shouted in warning.

Gabriel turned in time to see a bulky goblin barreling down on him. Before he could raise the Nimrod to defend himself, the goblin stopped short. A strange expression crossed his face, and he began clawing at something behind him. When he spun so that his back was to Gabriel, he saw the source of the goblin's discomfort. Mercy stood behind him, talons dug firmly into his back. With a grunt, she pulled out the goblin's spine along with a handful of his intestines.

"You're just determined to get us killed, aren't you?" she scolded Gabriel.

"We have to free them." He ignored her statement and continued looking for a way to open the cage.

Mercy shook her head. "Move." She shoved him out of the way. With two quick strikes from her talons, she had torn open the side of the cage. The slaves stampeded and bowled over one another with each trying to be the first to freedom.

"Mavis!" Cristobel rushed over and helped his sister from the cage first. He buried his hand in her hair and offered a prayer of thanks to the gods. "I thought I'd lost you."

"Had we made it to our destination, I fear you might've," Mavis said.

Redfeather was weak, but able to climb down from the cage unassisted. "My friend, it is good to see you survived," he greeted Cristobel. "Thank you for finding my grandson."

"He actually found us," Cristobel admitted.

"What's wrong with Lucy?" Gabriel noticed the witch sprawled on the floor of the cage. Even without the heightened sensitivity to magic the Nimrod granted him, he could tell something was wrong.

"She was poisoned by the venom of the Slov when we escaped the goblins in the forest," Cristobel filled them in.

"I was trying to help her when the goblins took us from the village," Mavis added.

Mercy snorted. "The smell of death clings to her. I fear this one is not long for this world."

Redfeather looked up, and for the first time he realized the Valkrin who had freed him from the cage hadn't been DeMona, but someone who he hadn't seen in ages. "Mercy?"

"Good to see you again, Redfeather." Her tone was less than convincing. At one time Mercy and her late husband, Edward, had considered Redfeather a friend, but much had changed since the days when she was masquerading as a human.

"I had heard rumors that you returned to the service of the Valkrin. I'm glad they were untrue," Redfeather said.

"They were quite true. Make no mistake, just because I've come here to aid my daughter in her foolish quest doesn't mean I've forgotten who or what I am," Mercy told him.

A solemn looked crossed Redfeather's face. "Mercy, I am sorry for the loss of your husband and all the other hardships that have turned your heart cold against mankind, but please don't forget who you were to us . . . to the order."

The struggle in Mercy's heart was apparent on her face. "What I was is a memory. What I am"—her hand shot up and plucked an arrow from the air that had been fired at Redfeather—"is a Valkrin warrior." She snapped the arrow in her hand. She turned to the younger Redfeather. "We've saved your people, Gabriel. Now let's leave this place while we still can." Mercy looked at the goblins inching ever closer. She knew the only thing that had kept them from swarming was fear of the Nimrod.

"You'll get no argument from me on that front," Jak said.

"What about the child?" Mavis asked.

Gabriel was confused. "What child?"

"There was a little girl on the other wagon inside that cube. We have to help her," Mavis said.

"We've already risked enough by coming here to rescue all of you. I'll not risk my life or that of my daughter for another human," Mercy said.

"Whatever she is, I don't think she's *human*," DeMona said. "That cube stunk of enchantment. I'm surprised your all-superior Valkrin nose didn't pick up on it," she taunted Mercy.

"I agree. Titus went through great lengths to make sure she was well guarded. I gather she is important to his plan somehow," Redfeather said.

"Then saving her may give us an edge. I'll go after the wagon and catch up with you guys as soon as I can," Gabriel volunteered.

"They've already gained too much ground. You're not fast enough, but I am," DeMona said.

"No, it's too dangerous. Leave the girl to her fate and let's go," Mercy ordered.

DeMona growled. "Stop trying to tell me what to do, *Mercy.*"

"I'm afraid none of you will be going anywhere." Illini stood between them and the fleeing wagon. Standing in close proximity, Gabriel could make out his deformed left arm. It looked to be a different size than the right and was scorched from fingertip to elbow as if someone had cooked it.

"The Executioner." Gilchrist trembled behind Gabriel's legs.

Illini looked down at Gilchrist and shook his head in disgust. "Greetings, little prince. I'd heard tales that you were a captive of the humans, yet I see no shackles. I wonder how Orden will take the news of your unfortunate passing."

"Death comes to he who touches a member of the royal family," Gilchrist hissed.

"True, but the rules do not apply if said family member is a traitor." Illini reached for Gilchrist with his blackened hand.

"Keep your distance, friend." Gabriel raised the trident threateningly.

Illini looked over Gabriel curiously. "I've heard tales of you, and forgive me if I offend, but the way Titus goes on about you, I'm not impressed. But what I think is insignificant. What's important is that my prince demands your head and your weapon." He turned to the goblins. "The boy is mine, the rest are meat. Kill them."

"You're the one who'll be dying today, goblin." Jak sprang forward with his twin blades.

"Don't!" Gilchrist tried to warn him, but it was too late.

Illini blocked Jak's strike with his long staff and grabbed him by the throat, lifting him off his feet. "I am a collector of things," he whispered, with his blackened hand slowly beginning to glow. "This"—he nodded at his hand—"I took from an elemental and claimed it as my own. What do you think of my hand of fire?" He laughed.

Jak struggled wildly as the skin around his neck began to smoke. Illini's deformed arm had been a trophy from a fire elemental he'd slain years prior. His hand flared, and Jak burst into flame. He tossed the dwarf to the ground and let his friends watch in horror as he burnt to a crisp.

"Jak!" Cristobel rushed to him and tried to use his cloak

to put out the flames. All that was left of his companion was a charred skeleton.

Illini opened his hand and blew the ash from his palm. "The sweet smell of cooked dwarf flesh. There is nothing quite like it."

"You'll pay for that, goblin." Cristobel raised his battle-axe and struck. Illini sidestepped the blow and grabbed a fistful of Cristobel's cloak. He had barely managed to free himself of it before it went up in flames. While he lay on the ground trying to compose himself, Illini moved in to finish him off with his hand of fire.

"No!" Gabriel charged. The trident flared brightly as he brought it down.

Illini blocked it with his long staff, and was thoroughly surprised at how strong the human was. "This may be more interesting than I thought." He shoved Gabriel backward, causing him to stumble into DeMona's arms.

"Let's kick his ass, Gabriel," DeMona snarled.

"No, save the girl from the wagon. I can take him," Gabriel told her.

"Are you sure?" DeMona asked.

"No, but we need to find out why that girl is so important to Titus. Just go," he barked.

DeMona looked from Gabriel to the advancing goblins. They were charging in a cluster like a football team wedge. She turned to her mother. "If you can clear a path, I can catch that wagon."

Mercy nodded. "Then a path you shall have." She called her demonic change and charged into the goblins, with De-Mona on her heels. Mother and daughter moved in an intricate dance, leaving a trail of blood and body parts as they cleaved through the goblin troop with claws and teeth. DeMona was merciless with her strikes, making just about every blow a fatal one. Though Mercy would never admit it, she was impressed with how well her daughter handled herself.

A goblin that stood easily nine feet barreled forward with murder in his eyes. Mercy was preoccupied with two smaller goblins, so she didn't see him until it was too late. He grabbed her from behind in a bear hug and began to squeeze. She struggled against him, but the goblin was too strong for even her Valkrin strength. "I will grind your bones to make my bread, traitor," he cackled in her ear.

"Let's see how you eat that bread with no teeth." Mercy threw her head back and smashed it into the goblin's mouth.

When the goblin dropped Mercy to attend to his injury, DeMona made her play. She launched herself into the air and swung at the goblin's neck with everything she had. Her claws paused for a heartbeat when they made contact with the goblin's skin, before continuing on through muscle and bone. The goblin's head spiraled from his shoulders like a missed field goal bouncing off a goalpost and landed in the dry earth.

"Are you okay?" DeMona knelt beside her mother to check her injuries. Seeing her mother fall, she momentarily forgot her resentment and was again just a daughter concerned for her mother.

"I'm fine. Get to the wagon," Mercy reminded her. DeMona paused before taking off after the little girl. Mercy watched the child she had abandoned rush off bravely into uncertain danger and couldn't help but feel her chest swell with pride. For as long as DeMona had been alive, Mercy had kept her sheltered from her true nature and the ways of war, but despite her best efforts, the blood of the Valkrin pumped through DeMona's veins and no one could deny that.

Bodies were strewn all over the battlefield. Mercy and Cristobel fought valiantly, decimating the goblin troop with steel and claw, but the few that remained were still very much in the fight. They held them at bay as best they could while in the center of the carnage the real battle had begun, as Gabriel and Illini squared off.

Gabriel's hands were slick with sweat, but his grip remained firm on the Nimrod. Occasionally he would cast a nervous glance over his shoulder to avoid getting blindsided by an overzealous goblin. Mercy and Cristobel held them off as best they could, but they all knew it was only a matter of time before reinforcements arrived and they were overrun. Gabriel needed to end this quickly.

"I smell the fear on you, human. No need to continue the brave act. Hand over the Nimrod, and I'll let you die on the battlefield instead of roasting on a spit," Illini taunted.

"Is it written somewhere in the supervillain handbook that all of you guys have to come up with cheesy threats?" Gabriel shot back. It was hardly the time to make jokes, but it was all he could do to suppress his ever-mounting fear.

One of the goblins made it past Mercy and Cristobel, and attacked Gabriel. Before he could react, Illini struck the goblin down with his long staff. He wrenched the pole in the fallen goblin's chest. "I will not be robbed of my glory."

Tiring of the dance, Illini lunged. He was so fast that Gabriel was only able to deflect half the blows he threw with his long staff. Illini struck Gabriel in the jaw with the end of his staff then followed with a blow to the gut, doubling him over. Before Gabriel could regain his balance, Illini whacked him across the butt and sent him spilling to the ground.

You'll never beat him that way, he's too skilled, but the Nimrod makes you more powerful. Use it! the Bishop urged.

Gabriel buried the shaft of the trident in the dirt and bid it to answer to him. In response, the Nimrod crackled with power and sent a surge of lightning through the ground. Illini's body went stiff as he was electrocuted. Pressing his advantage, Gabriel tackled Illini, sending the long staff skidding across the ground. Gabriel pinned Illini's arms to the ground with his knees and punched him in the face repeatedly.

"Are you impressed yet?" It was Gabriel's turn to taunt him.

Illini was able to free one of his arms and pressed his palm over Gabriel's chest, calling on his hand of fire. Gabriel howled in pain as a palm print was seared into his skin. Illini bucked and tossed Gabriel off him. Gabriel tried to get up, but an elbow to the spine sent him back down. Illini grabbed him by the front of the shirt and dragged him to his feet. "I am done toying with you, human. Now, you burn." He raised the hand of fire to Gabriel's face.

Gabriel felt a tingling in his arm and focused on it. Within seconds the Nimrod appeared in his hand. "You first." Gabriel drove the points of the trident through Illini's chin. Gabriel twisted the trident and with a sickening sound, Illini's head and body were separated. With Illini's head on the end of the Nimrod, Gabriel held it up for the goblins to see. "Behold your mighty leader." He flung the head, and it rolled to a stop in the middle of the goblins. "You have two choices: Live to fight another day or follow him into the Dead Lands." He pointed the Nimrod at them.

It was an easy choice. The goblins took off, trying to get

as far away from Gabriel and the Nimrod as possible. It was a possibility that they would be put to death for their cowardice, but it was a *fact* that they would die if they continued to fight. When the last of the goblins disappeared over the hills and the danger had passed, the trident returned to its resting place as the tattoo on Gabriel's arm and he rejoined his friends.

"Well done, General." Mercy gave him an approving nod.

Gabriel smirked weakly then continued on to his grandfather. "As soon as DeMona comes back, we're leaving. I have to get you to a hospital, and we've gotta find somebody to help Lucy."

"We'll take her to the White Queen. I can't say for sure how she'll receive us, but Lucy has a better chance with her own people than she does with us," Redfeather said.

"I agree." Gabriel nodded. "I'm going to go see what's keeping DeMona and then we're out of here." He took two steps and dropped to his knees, clutching his arm in pain.

Redfeather rushed to his side. "What's wrong? Are you hurt?"

"I don't know. It's like my arm is on fire." Gabriel rocked back and forth, cradling his arm. The Bishop was repeating a word over and over in his head, but Gabriel was so overwhelmed by the pain in his arm that he couldn't make out what he was saying. Whatever it was, he knew it wasn't good. "We need to get out of here, now." Gabriel staggered to his feet.

There was a commotion in the distance that drew all their attention. The same goblins that had just fled were now running back in their direction. Mercy and the others prepared for battle, but to their surprise, the goblins ran right past them.

"I wonder what's gotten into them," Cristobel said.

"Not what, but who." Redfeather looked to the top of the hill. There were dozens of goblins lining it, all armed and angry. Leading them was none other than the goblin prince.

• CHAPTER SIX •

DeMona's legs throbbed and her chest burned. She wasn't sure how much longer she would be able to keep it up. In her Valkrin form, she could run short distances at twice the speed of the fastest human, but she had never pushed it this far. She had been in a flat-out sprint for over a mile, chasing the wagon and its cargo.

A few yards ahead of her, she could see the dust cloud being kicked up by the armored wagon. Beyond that was their destination, a tower made of what looked like black stones. She knew there would be more goblins at the tower, and if she allowed them to reach it, she didn't stand a chance of rescuing the girl.

DeMona forced herself to go faster, faster than she had ever run in her life. She kept pushing until she was within arm's reach of the wagon. She could see the driver peer back at her and shout something to someone sitting next to him, whom she couldn't see. It didn't take her long to find out who it was, as a goblin crawled atop the wagon with a crossbow. He fired two quick shots, both of which missed DeMona but altered her course enough to slow her down.

"To hell with this," DeMona spat. She leapt forward and slashed the back wheel of the wagon with her claws, before crashing face-first into the dirt. She looked up in time to see the wagon begin to wobble, before eventually falling over on its side.

The cube toppled from the wagon, and tumbled end over end until it came to a stop. Whatever it was made of, it couldn't have been glass because it didn't break during the fall, but the tarp fell away and revealed what, or who, was inside. She was a girl of no more than eleven or twelve with soft pink hair and pale skin that almost shimmered with magic. Redfeather was right; she was definitely not human. The little girl's molten gold eyes landed on DeMona and seemed to call to her. Without explanation, DeMona suddenly had the overwhelming urge to save the girl at all costs.

DeMona gathered herself on hands and knees in time to see the two goblins from the wagon advancing on her, one with sword and one with crossbow. She faked as if she were more severely injured than she actually was, drawing them closer. Their eyes lit up when they realized their quarry was a Valkrin, and their anxiousness to bring her head back to their prince overrode their caution. When they were right on top of her, DeMona struck.

There was a shower of steel and blood as DeMona's talons shattered the goblin's blade before tearing through his face. With her second strike, his head flew from his shoulders. The crossbow-wielding goblin tried to run, but DeMona overtook him. She grabbed him from behind by the corners of his mouth and pulled until the skin ripped up both sides of his face, leaving his jawbone and lower teeth exposed. With a wrench of her powerful hands, she broke his neck and put him out of his misery. Still caught in battle frenzy, she looked around frantically for another opponent but there was none.

Still in full Valkrin form, DeMona approached the cube holding the little girl. She had expected the child to recoil at the site of her, but she didn't. Her golden eyes took in DeMona, displaying more fascination than fear. "I'm going to get you out of there," she assured the girl while searching the cube for some type of door. When she couldn't find a way to open it, she got frustrated. "What is this, some kind of trick box where I need a magic word to open it?"

The girl spoke. *It's enchanted, forged of magic and warded against magic. No spell can open it.*

DeMona was startled because even with her heightened hearing, there should've been no way she could've heard the girl through the airtight glass. It was then that she realized she wasn't hearing the girl's words, but her thoughts. "How did you—"

There's no time, the girl cut her off. *Already the goblins' reinforcements march to reclaim me. Hurry, please.*

"Move back," DeMona told her while raising her hands high above her head.

I told you that the box cannot be opened by magic, the girl reminded her.

"I don't plan on using magic, just good old-fashioned American muscle." DeMona crashed one of her fists into the box. When her fist made contact, she could feel whatever it was that protected the box fighting against her, but she would not be outdone. Cupping her hands like a hammer, she swung with all her might, shattering the glass.

The girl jumped back, careful not to get caught in the

shower of glass. She looked up at the Valkrin as if DeMona were going to eat her.

DeMona extended her hand. "It's okay. I'm not going to hurt you. C'mon out, kid."

The little girl was hesitant but eventually took DeMona's hand and stepped from the box. She took a deep breath. The air was stale and dry, but it was the first time in a very long time that she had inhaled air that wasn't artificial.

"You got a name, kid?" DeMona asked.

"Yes, I am called Leah."

"Well, I'm DeMona." She extended her hand. Instead of shaking it, Leah wrapped her thin arms around DeMona's waist and gave her hug.

"Thank you so much. I thought I would be locked in that box forever and had it not been for you, I likely would have." She began to weep. Her tears looked like golden sparkles coming down her face.

"You don't have to cry, Leah. You're free now. Why did Titus have you locked away like that anyhow?" DeMona asked.

"Because of what I am," she said.

"And what exactly are you?" DeMona asked. She was not new to the supernatural world, but had never encountered anyone like Leah.

Leah hesitated. "I am a sprite, sometimes you call us fairies. Titus was trying to force me to use my powers to help him in his sick plan, but I refused, so he imprisoned me." She began sobbing again. It was a half-truth, but enough of the truth so DeMona wouldn't be suspicious of her.

"Well, that's the end of his little plan, and for as long as I'm around, you'll never be locked away again," DeMona declared. She never gave a second thought as to why she felt so protective over a child she had just met.

Both their eyes shifted to the horizon when they heard someone approaching. DeMona could see something in the distance coming their way incredibly fast. At first, she thought it was more of the goblin riders on their mutated animals until she recognized the sound of a car engine. As the object got closer, she realized it was an SUV. When she recognized the symbol etched on it, she let out a whoop.

"What is it?" Leah asked nervously.

"The cavalry," DeMona told her and went to meet the vehicle. "Boy, are you a sight for sore eyes," she greeted Rogue when he climbed from behind the wheel of the Hummer.

"Good to see you too, kid." Rogue embraced her.

"How did you get here? Wait, a better question is, how the heck did you get that here?" DeMona pointed at the Hummer.

Rogue winked at her from behind his shades. "I have my ways. Where are the others?"

"About a mile or so north of here. They held off the goblins while I rescued her." DeMona nodded toward Leah.

When Rogue looked at the little girl, his shadow eyes picked up on something very powerful. He tried to hone in on what it was, but something clouded his vision and when it passed, she looked like a harmless child again.

"John, must I remind you that time is not our friend?" Gilgamesh called from the passenger window in a not-so-friendly tone.

"Friend of yours?" DeMona asked.

"Unfortunately yes, but pay him no mind. What Gilgamesh lacks in people skills, he more than makes up for on the battlefield. Let's get you two in the Hummer so we can get the rest of our people and get the hell out of here."

DeMona led Leah by the hand to the idling Hummer. Rogue continued to stare at the little girl, trying to place his finger on what was off about her. He peered over his shades and tried to focus his shadow eyes on what she was hiding when something akin to being slapped jarred him. Leah gave a playful look over her shoulder at the stunned mage before climbing into the vehicle.

· CHAPTER SEVEN ·

Orden," Gilchrist said in a trembling tone.

Orden was a monster of a creature, even for a goblin. He stood over seven feet tall and resembled a hairless gorilla with his muscular frame and arms that stretched nearly to the ground. Fangs jutted from behind his bottom lip and tickled his top short tusks. A single braid hung from his large bald head, with a spear tip woven into it at the end. His cold blue eyes drank in the group of invaders, but stopped on Gilchrist.

"Greetings, little brother. I'm not sure if I am pleased or disappointed that the rumors of your demise are untrue." Orden spoke in a low, gravelly tone.

Gilchrist rushed forward and threw himself at Orden's feet. "Oh, mighty prince, glad to see you, Gilchrist is. Thought I would forever be prisoner, I did."

Orden kicked the smaller goblin, sending him rolling back

down the hill. "I'll just bet. You and I will have words later, little brother. Right now . . ." Orden's words trailed off when he spotted Illini's headless body. He rumbled down the hill and knelt next to the corpse, cradling it in his arms. He and Illini had been friends since they were children trying to earn their fathers' favors on the battlefield, and his death rocked the goblin prince. Orden let out a roar that seemed to shake the very mountains. After offering up a prayer to the gods of war for Illini, he turned his rage-filled blue eyes to his troops.

"Listen well, my brothers." He drew the two sabers from the scabbards strapped to his back. "Goblin blood has been drawn by outsiders, and by our oldest laws and traditions, the offenders are meat for the horde!"

"Sorry, but I don't think I want to be on your dinner menu tonight." Mercy drew her sword and lunged. She crashed her fists into Orden's jaw with enough force to pulverize a brick wall, but only succeeded in stumbling the goblin prince.

Orden spat on the ground and was surprised to see blood in his saliva. He turned his blue eyes back to Mercy and smiled. "I'm going to savor sucking the marrow from your traitorous bones."

Within seconds, the sounds of battle rang out all over, and blood stained the earth. Gabriel and Cristobel stood back to back, protecting their loved ones against the advancing goblins. Gabriel dragged the points of the Nimrod through the dirt in a wide circle around them, and then called the lightning. From the ground sprang a wall of electricity that stood between friends and foes. One brave, yet foolish, goblin tested the barrier and found himself incinerated, which made the rest hesitant to try their luck, but it was only a temporary reprieve.

Soon the goblins' fear of failing their prince would override their fear of the electric wall, and Gabriel and his friends would be overrun.

Redfeather came to stand beside Gabriel. In his good hand, he held a sword he'd retrieved from one of the goblin corpses. The weight of the blade showed in his trembling arm, but he never let it drop an inch under his shoulder. "Lucy is unconscious, and I am wounded. We're liabilities. I'll hold them off while you escape."

"You know I'm not going to leave you down here to die," Gabriel told him.

"Gabriel, for as much as I hate to admit it, the thing that has attached itself to you may be the best chance that humanity has. The lives that will be lost down here are insignificant weighed against those you may be able to save if you live to continue the fight. Take the dwarves and go!"

"How so very like a Redfeather, ready to throw your life away for the greater good. I see that all-damning sense of nobility hasn't been diluted through the years." A man stepped from the throng of goblins. He appeared to be somewhere in his early forties with dark hair and a dark goatee both sprinkled with salt and pepper. Dressed in a suit and black gloves, he looked completely out of place among the goblins. Slung across his hip was a sword with a jeweled handle. His hand rested on the sword, but he didn't move to draw it.

Gabriel had never set eyes on the man before, but he felt like he knew him and not in a good way. His heart was suddenly filled with rage, and he had an overwhelming desire to kill the stranger. It was then that he was able to decipher the word that the Bishop had been chanting over and over in his head. "Betrayer!" he hissed.

"I've been called worse," Titus said with an easy smile. He

approached the barrier, and instead of being electrocuted like the others, he easily passed through and stood mere feet from Gabriel. This was the closest he had been to the Nimrod in centuries and the piece of it lodged in his chest throbbed as painfully as Gabriel's arm, but he didn't show it. "At last we meet, or should I say meet again?"

Gabriel could feel the presence of the Bishop deep within his subconscious, raging and beating against the walls of his mind. When he opened his mouth to reply, it was his voice, but not his words. "And on this day, I will give the ferrymen the life you cheated him out of four centuries ago."

Titus drew his sword. "Or grant me the glory I was denied when your cowardly soul retreated into the Nimrod. Let's finish it."

"With pleasure." Gabriel sprang forward. When the Nimrod made contact with Titus's blade, there was a great flash of power that knocked both combatants back. They clashed again, sending off sparks each time their weapons collided. Gabriel tried to plunge the Nimrod into Titus's chest, but he deflected each strike with his sword and forced him backward.

Titus's lips were twisted into a smirk, while a playful light glinted in his eyes as he stalked Gabriel, holding his sword aloof but ready. "I would've thought you'd at least have picked a more fitting physical specimen to host your great return, Bishop."

"It was the hands of a Redfeather who struck you down the first time, and it will be the hands of a Redfeather who puts you down for good." Gabriel whipped out his hand and sent a bolt of lightning streaking at Titus.

Titus raised his hand and absorbed the bolt. "I'm impressed, but it'll take more than a light show to save your life." Titus threw the bolt back at him.

Gabriel's body convulsed as the electricity ran through it,

dazing him. Before the fog could lift from his mind, Titus hit him with an uppercut that sent him flying. He brought the sword down, but Gabriel scrambled out of the way. He got back to his feet, but was in no rush to reengage Titus. He had stood against many evils over the past few days, but none of them radiated the same menace that Titus did. It was like his very presence was smothering, and it had him unnerved.

Your fear will be your undoing. Stand up to him, the Bishop said.

Gabriel ignored the Bishop and kept his focus on Titus. The half-demon feigned high and went low, intending to gut Gabriel, but the lithe boy danced out of the way at the last second and struck Titus behind the ear with the shaft of the Nimrod.

Titus touched his fingers behind his ear and was surprised when they came away bloody. "Maybe you won't die as easily as I had anticipated."

Gabriel sneered. "The fact that your people have been trying their hardest to kill me and I'm here to talk shit to you about it should attest to my will to live."

You are no match for Titus, boy. Release me and I will slay him! the Bishop demanded.

"If you think I'm foolish enough to give you free rein of my body, then you're crazier than everyone says you are," Gabriel whispered to the Bishop.

Titus struck while Gabriel was distracted, and if it hadn't been for the rock behind him tripping Gabriel, he would've lost his head. He spilled to the ground just as Titus's blade whistled through the air. Never breaking his motion, Titus stabbed the blade downward trying to pierce Gabriel's heart, but he rolled out of the way a hair's breadth before it dug into the dirt.

Gabriel spun to his feet and swung the trident backhanded

at Titus's face, but Titus grabbed his wrist midswing. Gabriel struggled, but the half-demon was too strong. Titus turned Gabriel's wrist until he heard the bones pop. The trident fell from his hand and clattered to the ground.

"Humans are so fragile." Titus hit him in the gut and made Gabriel cough blood. Gabriel swung with his free hand, but Titus swatted it away. He wrenched Gabriel's wrist farther, and the pain brought him to his knees. "If you are all that stands between me and conquering the mortal world, then they are doomed." He kicked Gabriel in the chest and sent him skidding across the ground.

Gabriel wanted to pass out, but the pain in his arm wouldn't let him. The Bishop shouted commands at him in his head, but his voice was as weak as Gabriel's body felt. His head lolled to the side, and he took in the scene playing out like slow-motion movie frames. Mercy was holding her own against Orden, but the same couldn't be said for Cristobel and the elder Redfeather. The wall of electricity had fallen, and the goblins were closing in. All would be lost unless Gabriel did something.

Gabriel grunted his teeth against the pain and reached for the Nimrod, willing it to come to him. The trident rattled on the ground before sliding through the dirt in his direction. It was almost within his reach, until Titus's heavy boot came down and stopped it.

When Titus picked the Nimrod up, he immediately felt the rush of power. Even four hundred years later, it still made him giddy as a school child. "Is this what you wanted?" He held it for Gabriel to see before plunging the points into his leg. "Tell me, how does its points feel ripping into your skin as it did mine all those years ago?" He twisted the trident, drawing a howl of pain from Gabriel. He ripped the bloody trident from Gabriel's leg and held it high for the final strike. "This time, I'm going to make sure you stay dead."

At the same time Titus brought the Nimrod down, an inky blackness pooled beneath Gabriel and he was sucked into the earth. Titus stood there dumbfounded, but before he could make sense of it, he found himself blinded by light.

· CHAPTER EIGHT ·

Rogue whipped the Hummer expertly over the rough terrain of the Iron Mountains. It wasn't his Viper, but he could handle anything with wheels. From his days of driving getaway cars for his homies when they pulled capers, to the high-speed chases when he was a part of the Florida Police Department, Rogue had always been a driver. Gilgamesh sat in the passenger seat, and Teko in the seat directly behind him. DeMona and the little girl, who had been introduced as Leah, occupied the last row. It seemed like every time Rogue looked in the rearview mirror, he could see her golden eyes looking back at him.

"We left them just over this hill," DeMona called up from the back row.

"Good, let's get your people and get out of here," Gilgamesh said, adjusting the two black gauntlets he wore on his hands.

"Teko, be ready to open a rip immediately, because we'll be leaving *fast*."

There was the sound of thunder in the distance, followed by a flash of light coming from just beyond the hill they were headed toward. Leah let out a blood-curdling scream that startled everyone in the Hummer. She whipped her head back and forth, covering her ears as if she could hear some terrible sound that was muted to everyone else.

DeMona clutched the girl to her reassuringly. "Leah, what's wrong?"

"The apocalypse has begun," she sobbed.

Rogue was about to ask her what she meant, but the Hummer cleared the hill and he saw for himself. From what DeMona had told them, they expected to encounter a few goblins, but what lay before them looked like half of the goblin horde, led by Orden himself. That was surprising, but what was more surprising was seeing Titus. He and Gabriel were locked in a fierce battle, and from what Rogue could tell, Gabriel was getting the short end of the stick. If he fell to Titus, then escaping the Iron Mountains would no longer be a problem because they would no longer have a world to escape to.

DeMona spotted her mother fighting with Orden. She was holding her own against him until she was swarmed by goblins. Mercy was a formidable warrior, but even she didn't stand a chance against those odds. "I've got to help her." She climbed from the back seat.

Teko grabbed her by the arm. "Don't be foolish. There are too many of them. The Valkrin are warriors and to die in battle is a great honor for them."

DeMona jerked away. "That isn't just some Valkrin; it's my mother."

"Wait a second, DeMona!" Rogue called to her, but she

had already disappeared through the sunroof of the Hummer. "Dumb kid is gonna get us killed."

"I told you that throwing in your lot with them was a fool's mission. Let's kill Titus, and get out of here. Leave them to their own devices."

"You know I can't do that, Mesh. Take the wheel." Before Gilgamesh could protest, Rogue melted into shadow and seeped out through the window.

Gilgamesh barely had time to jump in the driver's seat and take control of the vehicle to save them from crashing. "Curse you and your bleeding heart, John."

"Shall I go after them?" Teko asked.

"No, if Rogue and his buddies wanna be passengers on the *Jihad* tonight, it's their choice. We're gonna skip that trip," Gilgamesh told him. The *Jihad* was the ghost ship that ferried souls to the Dead Lands. "I'm going to take Titus out, then we're leaving, with or without Rogue."

When Leah laughed from the back seat, it sounded like tinkling bells. Her golden eyes stared back at Gilgamesh in the rearview mirror. "You either underestimate your enemy or overestimate your own skill. Either would make you a fool, dark elf. Titus is strong in the mortal world, but the magic of Midland doubles his demonic power. Try to take him alone, and you will fall," she said in a tone that was thick with power.

Gilgamesh met her gaze in the mirror. "Maybe, but before I fall, I'm going to make sure I knock him down." He pressed on the gas. His eyes were locked on Titus, who hovered over Gabriel with the trident. Thoughts of his uncle and cousin filled his mind and made him press harder on the gas, picking up speed. When he was almost on top of them, he saw the ground swallow Gabriel, leaving a clear path to Titus.

"My uncle Croft sends his regards from the Dead Lands!" he screamed before running Titus down.

Orden moved with the speed of a man half his size. His hands were like blurs, swinging the sabers at Mercy. Every time she blocked one with her sword, she could feel the vibrations running up her arms. Orden swung the sabers overhand, and she raised her sword to block them. Their blades locked while the two combatants danced in a circle, each trying to gain leverage. She delivered a knee to Orden's stomach, doubling him over and exposing his neck. Mercy brought her blade around to take his head, but before it could connect, an arrow whistled through the air, striking the sword and knocking it out of her hand.

With her lips drawn back into a snarl, she looked over her shoulder and saw one of the goblins reloading his bow with an arrow. "Before this is done, you're gonna pay for that," she assured him. When she turned her attention back to Orden, the world exploded into bright stars as his brutish fist slammed into her chin and put her on her back. Before she could get back to her feet, she felt the press of steel on both sides of her neck.

Orden grinned down at her. "They say that the blood of the Valkrin is like bitter wine, and I intend to get quite drunk tonight."

There was a feral growl behind him. Orden turned in time to see the younger Valkrin hurling through the air in his direction with her claws bared before the sky exploded in bright shades of red.

———

Mercy heard a scream, right before blood splattered into her eyes, temporarily blinding her. When she was able to see again, it was a welcome sight. Orden danced around, howling in pain with one of his meaty hands covering his bloody face. Kneeling a few feet away from him was the cause of his misery.

DeMona crouched, heaving as if she had just run a marathon. Fangs jutted from her upper lip, and the spine of bones that ran along her temples was fully raised. It was the first time Mercy had ever seen her in her full Valkrin form, and she was as beautiful as the day she had come into the world. Her arms were crossed in front of her, blood dripping onto the earth from her balled fists. She held one of her hands out for Mercy to see what was hiding in her palm. It was Orden's bloody eyeball.

Orden removed his hand, exposing the mangled hole where his eye once rested. His remaining eye was filled with rage and locked on DeMona. "Demon, a swift death is too good for you. I think I will let every man in my horde defile your body before I tear out your still beating heart."

Mercy and DeMona stood shoulder to shoulder while Orden lumbered toward them, saber in hand and murder in his heart.

"It is every Valkrin's dream to stand side by side on the field of battle with their daughters, but it was never mine. I wanted you to know a life without war," Mercy admitted.

"And I wanted a family, but I guess, so much for what we want," DeMona said. "So, we gonna stand here reenacting *Steel Magnolias* or we gonna kill this bastard?"

Mercy called on her full change, with her body bulking up to almost twice the size it had been. "Spoken like a true Valkrin."

"Nah, spoken like a true Sanchez," DeMona corrected her before throwing herself at Orden.

The goblin prince swung his blade wildly trying to fall the two demons who moved in what looked like an orchestrated dance, opening up cuts and gashes on every part of Orden's exposed flesh that their claws could touch. Mercy was skillful in her strikes, but DeMona was driven by rage.

DeMona went to take Orden's legs out from under him, but he sidestepped her and grabbed a fistful of her hair. DeMona slashed at his thighs and legs, opening up nasty wounds, but he held fast to her hair. Orden whipped DeMona in the air like a rag doll and brought her back to the ground violently over and over again, until a clump of her hair tore away and freed her. DeMona was in a world of pain, but her Valkrin nature wouldn't allow her to stay down. She managed to crawl into a kneeling position and through dazed eyes saw Orden's saber speeding for her heart.

There was a blur just outside her line of vision, then Mercy appeared between DeMona and Orden. The tip of the blade that had been meant for DeMona plunged deep into Mercy's chest and came out through her back, mere inches from DeMona's face.

Mercy looked up at Orden with defiant eyes before she thrust both her claws into his sides, shredding his organs. Fighting against the pain, she began pulling him closer to her and driving the blade deeper into her chest. "Take him." Mercy coughed blood.

DeMona sprang to her feet and lashed out with her talons. Her bladed fingernails sliced through leathery skin and impossibly thick muscle before striking bone. She took a firm grip on Orden's spine and ripped it, along with his head, from his body. When Orden's carcass hit the ground, it was like the shot heard round the world and the goblins stopped. They all looked on in shock at what was left of their fallen leader and the young girl who had slain him.

· CHAPTER NINE ·

Rogue moved through the Shadow Lands like a torpedo. He knew that traveling so fast through the collective could potentially draw him some unwanted attention, but he didn't have the time to be cautious. He needed to reach Gabriel and get him out of harm's way ASAP.

In the Shadow Lands, he didn't have physical senses like sight or sound, but the collective awareness of the shadows was connected to all things. Just ahead of him, he could feel the draw of two distinct energies, both intense. Knowing it had to be Gabriel and Titus giving them off, he moved in that direction. Rogue had never attempted what he was about to do, and he hoped that it didn't result in both their deaths, but he had little other choice. If Titus slew Gabriel, they were all as good as dead anyway.

Tearing himself away from the collective, Rogue pushed toward the light. He used his will to spread the shadows, opening a pool just beneath Gabriel and Titus. Concentrating on Gabriel, he pulled him through the veil. The boy sank into the shadows like a stone sinking in glue. Pulling a mortal through the Shadow Lands was like trying to pull a small car, because of their inability to change their body densities. Rogue didn't need to get him far, just out of reach of Titus, so they could reemerge in the light. But he had to do it quick. Gabriel's presence upset the balance of the Shadow Lands, and it would only be a matter of time before the dark things were drawn to them like sharks to blood. Rogue could already feel a presence moving toward him. It was massive and malevolent.

The presence drew ever closer to Rogue while he tried his best to make it back into the light before it caught up with him. He could feel the presence take hold of Gabriel's prone body and try to pull him back down, but Rogue held fast. He had intended on easing Gabriel back into the light as he had eased him into the shadows so as not to hurt him, but he had to throw caution to the wind or risk losing him to the presence that had descended on them. Giving it everything he had, Rogue pushed and propelled himself and Gabriel through the shadow veil and into the light.

Rogue lay there in the dirt for a few minutes, trying to reorient himself. Even with his connection to the demon he had gotten his eyes from, traveling through the Shadow Lands was always physically taxing on his body, which is why he only did it under the most extreme circumstances. Each time he bonded with the collective in that way, it was at the risk of losing his free will for good, so he was always cautious of how much of himself he gave to the shadows.

When the side effects of his trip had passed, Rogue risked getting to his feet and trying to get his bearings. Gabriel lay splayed prone on the ground. For a minute he'd thought he'd accidentally killed him, until he saw his chest rising and falling softly. He was kneeling beside the youth trying to revive him, when he felt the presence again that he had felt in the Shadow Lands. He turned in time to see a pool of shadow ooze from the ground and coagulate into the form of a man.

"We meet again, puppet," Moses said. "This time——"

Before he could finish his sentence, Rogue whipped out his revolver with the enchanted bullets from the holster and put two slugs between Moses's eyes, scattering his oily remains. "Yup, heard that one before."

Gabriel gasped like a drowning man when he emerged from the darkness. Not sure where he was, his head whipped back and forth trying to get his bearings. Everything was hazy, like he had just awakened from a short nap, but the chill in his bones ushered the grogginess away. He tried to push himself off the ground, but collapsed back down in pain when his broken arm reminded him of what he had just gone through.

"Don't try to move just yet, kid. Take a few minutes to let your body adjust," Rogue urged him.

"What happened? How did I get here?" Gabriel was confused.

"What happened is that I cheated the reaper out of his due, but I had to bring you through the Shadow Lands to do it. Even with my buddy passes"—he pointed to his eyes—"traveling through the Shadow Lands is like a bad hangover, so I can't imagine how you're feeling."

Gabriel got up off the ground. His legs were a little unsteady but held fast. "I feel like crap, but I guess better that than dead. I owe you . . . again."

"Yeah, you do, but I'm not keeping score," Rogue said. "Where's the Nimrod?"

"Titus took it," Gabriel said shamefully.

"Then we need to get it back or all this will be for nothing. How bad are you hurt?"

"I think my arm is broken," Gabriel told him.

"Okay, but since you're standing, I'm assuming that you can walk, so let's go," Rogue urged him forward toward the battle.

The Hummer sat on three wheels with Titus's body under the fourth wheel, prone. A few feet away the Nimrod lay, reverted to the broken pitchfork it had been when DeMona first brought it to Gabriel. Gilgamesh climbed from the driver's side window while Teko pulled Leah out through the busted back window. Rogue and Gabriel arrived at the wreck about the same time DeMona and Mercy did.

"Glad to see you're still with us, *General*," Mercy greeted Gabriel.

"I could say the same. Where's Orden?" Gabriel asked.

"Waiting around for the vultures to come pick at his corpse," DeMona answered.

"Slain Orden, you have?" Gilchrist asked in shock.

"It was either him or us," DeMona said. She had expected him to make a stink, or possibly even try to take revenge for his brother's murder, but to her surprise, he started laughing.

"Many seasons, joke of the goblin court, I have been. Abused by Orden, I was. Now, him dead, and Gilchrist prince of goblins." The little goblin clapped his hands excitedly.

"Well, congratulations on your promotion. For as much as we would love to stay for your coronation, I think its best we get out of here. Looks like the shock of seeing their prince missing his head has worn off and your buddies look pissed."

DeMona pointed at the goblins that were advancing on them.

"No need to run, you have. I'm new goblin prince, and horde must listen to me. Him"—he pointed to Gabriel—"save Gilchrist life. A debt owed, there is. And now I settle it." Gilchrist came around the side of the Hummer and addressed the approaching goblins. "Hear me well, brothers of the Iron Mountains. Dead is our prince Orden, and I, Gilchrist, now command the horde. As my first order—" Gilchrist was cut off when he was snatched under the Hummer. There were sounds of struggle, and a few seconds later, Gilchrist's body shot out from under the vehicle and rolled to a stop at DeMona's feet. When his limp head rolled to the side, she could see the chunk of flesh that had been torn from his throat.

Mavis rushed to the Gilchrist's side and started tending his wound. She tore off a piece of her skirt and wrapped it around his neck, packing it with dirt to slow the bleeding, but the wound was too deep. Still Mavis kept trying.

"Cold, am I. Dying, I fear," Gilchrist said. His voice was distorted as some of his vocal cords had been mangled.

"You're not dying, now hush and let me work," Mavis told him.

One of the goblins broke from the horde and stepped forward. Cristobel immediately moved to protect his sister, battle-axe ready. The goblin raised his hands, showing he meant no harm. Gilchrist hissed at the goblin, but didn't have the strength to stop him when he placed his hands over Mavis's to try and contain the flow of blood.

"Bound for the Dead Lands, I am, yes?" Gilchrist asked the goblin. The goblin nodded. "Blade!"

When the goblin removed his dagger and made to hand it

to Gilchrist, Mavis swatted it away. "He doesn't need a weapon. He needs medical attention."

"No!" Gilchrist croaked. "To die empty-handed is shame. Let I board the *Jihad* with blade in hand as ancestors did." He reached for the dagger. This time, Mavis let the goblin give it to him without protest. Gilchrist touched the steel to his cheek, and it seemed to soothe him. "For centuries, blind hate between dwarves and goblins, but Gilchrist see clearly now, thanks to girl. When I pass to the Dead Lands, curses for dwarves will not stain my lips, but praises for she." He touched Mavis's hand. In the end, the wound was too deep, and there was nothing Mavis or anyone else could do for him. In the shadow of the Iron Mountains, the only home Gilchrist had ever known, he took his last breaths.

Long after Gilchrist had stopped breathing, Mavis continued to try to revive him. Cristobel was finally able to pull her to her feet, and she broke down sobbing. "There was nothing I could do." She buried her face into her brother's chest.

Cristobel tried to soothe her. "Don't blame yourself, sister."

The goblin who had tried to help stared at her curiously. "Why?" he blurted out.

"Why what?" Cristobel asked.

"Dwarves and goblins enemies, and he goblin prince. Why help instead of letting him die?"

Mavis turned to the goblin with tear-filled eyes. "Because unlike the horde, we understand the value of life, dwarf or goblin."

The goblin stood there for a while, weighing her words. He nodded in understanding. "Goblins and dwarves enemies since the beginning and will be enemies in the end, but no more bloodshed tonight. Tonight, we honor our dead princes.

Tomorrow, goblins and dwarfs kill each other again." He started in the direction of the horde to deliver his decree.

The Hummer unexpectedly began rocking back and forth before it flipped over, and Titus crawled from the wreckage. The skin on his face was ripped and bloodied, but already starting to heal. Still clutching his sword, he wiped the smear of goblin blood from the side of his mouth. "There will be no truces this night," he told the goblin. "Rally your troops and kill the invaders."

The goblin approached Titus and looked at him defiantly. "You have no say here, halfling. Both our princes and our general are dead. I command the goblin horde, and I say the fighting for today is done."

Titus raised his eyebrow. "Is that so?" Almost faster than anyone's eyes could follow, he swung his blade and took the goblin's head. He then turned and addressed the horde. "You can either follow me into battle or wait for your turn to die when I control all of Midland. Make your choice." There was a brief discussion among what remained of the horde before they all drew arms and flocked behind Titus. Just as quickly as the truce had been struck, it was broken.

"So much for peace talks," DeMona said sarcastically.

"We've done enough talking. It's time for bloodshed!" Gilgamesh threw his cloak back, revealing the two gauntlets that stretched from knuckle to elbow. "Die, halfling!" he shouted, before activating the gauntlets. Small arrows fired from his wrists with the velocity of machine guns, dotting Titus from thigh to chest.

Titus looked down at the dark arrows protruding from his body. They sank into his skin, with the wounds healing over behind them. His lips drew back into a grin. "My turn." He touched his blade to one of the lava pools, and it caught fire. Titus lashed out with the blade, sending a stream of fire at Gilgamesh.

Rogue materialized from the shadows and tackled Gilgamesh out of the way before he was incinerated. Still in midflight, Rogue fired with his enchanted revolver, opening quarter-sized holes in Titus's chest. The enchanted bullets were more effective than Gilgamesh's arrows, but they still wouldn't be enough to stop Titus.

"Teko, the rip!" Gilgamesh shouted.

The Gammurai waved his glowing sword in a complex pattern before slicing through air. There was a tear that appeared suspended before them and widened the brighter Teko's blade burned. On the other side of the tear, they could see the scrap yard.

"Get your people out of here. I'm not done with Titus," Gilgamesh said.

"Mesh, don't be stupid. If Titus doesn't get us, the goblins will. We've got to regroup," Rogue told him.

"But my uncle—"

"Is dead and gone," Rogue cut him off. "You'll not be able to honor his memory if you're in a grave next to his. Let's live to fight another day."

"Fine, but I will have my reckoning," Gilgamesh vowed, heading toward the rip with the others.

Rogue covered their exit, trying to singlehandedly hold off their enemies. Titus sent a wave of fire at him, but Rogue was able to melt into shadow before it connected and reappeared a few feet away, blasting away with the enchanted revolver. Seeing Titus had given the goblins renewed courage, and they came in force. Rogue blasted away, dropping them with the powerful lead slugs, but there were far more goblins than he had bullets and all that the enchanted rounds he was pumping into Titus seemed to do was slow him down. When both his guns clicked empty, Rogue resorted to shadow magic. He sent a wave of shadow across the ground, which acted like super glue, stopping his enemies in their tracks. He had bought them some time, but not much.

Teko stood at the mouth of the rip, holding it open for the others to pass through. Gilgamesh was through first, in case there were any unexpected surprises waiting for them on the other side. Once the coast was clear, he waved the others through. Mavis went through next, leading Leah by the hand, followed by Cristobel. Mercy carried Lucy's prone body over her shoulder, while DeMona acted as a crutch to help the elder Redfeather to the mouth of the rip, where they would wait their turns to pass. Gabriel lingered for a while, waiting for Rogue to catch up.

He saw the mage sprinting in their direction, with Titus hot on his heels. He ducked and dodged as Titus hurled fireballs at him, trying his best to slay the mage and keep them from escaping. One of the fireballs landed in front of Rogue, exploding and knocking him down.

"Rogue!" Gabriel rushed to his side.

"Kid, you gotta get out of here." Rogue shoved him away.

"You came back for me, so I'm not leaving you." Gabriel helped Rogue to his feet as best he could with his injured arm and together they limped the rest of the way toward the rip.

"The only escape for you is when the wind scatters your charred ashes," Titus snarled. He called the fire again and launched it.

Rogue and Gabriel hit the ground to avoid the fireball, but

to their surprise, it sailed right past them. He wasn't aiming for them, but the rip. DeMona shoved Redfeather to the ground, and they narrowly escaped the fireball that exploded at the mouth of the rip. Teko wasn't so lucky. They watched in horror as flames engulfed his body and his sword fell to the ground. Without Teko, the magic began to fade and with it, the rip and any chance they had of escaping the Iron Mountains.

Rogue rolled over on his back and lashed out with the shadows. Tendrils of darkness sprang from the ground and bound Titus's arms and legs. Rogue pulled at them like reins on a horse and Titus fell onto his face. While he was down, Rogue wrapped him from ankle to head in shadow.

"Do you think that will stop him?" Gabriel asked nervously.

Rogue looked at the shadow mummy which had already begun to smoke and burn away. "Nope, so let's move!"

Rogue and Gabriel ran toward the rip where DeMona and Redfeather urged them through. Mercy went through, followed by Rogue. As an afterthought Rogue whipped out a shadow tendril and pulled Teko's blade through the rip behind him. The blade was useless without Teko, but it was all that was left of him, and he figured Gilgamesh might want it for sentimental reasons. He and Teko were as close as he and Rogue, possibly closer because of how long they had been together.

Gabriel was the last to step into the rip. He was making his way to the other side when something tripped him up. An invisible force had taken hold of his ankle and was pulling him back toward Midland. Glancing over his shoulder, he saw Titus had freed himself from the shadows that bound him.

"I will not be denied," Titus declared, tugging at the invisible cord.

Rogue and DeMona grabbed Gabriel by the arms and tried to pull him free, but Titus was too strong.

"Leave me, I'm only gonna get all of us killed!" Gabriel shouted.

"Nothing doing, Gabriel." DeMona fought to keep her grip on him. Another fireball sailed through the air and shattered into burning embers against the rip. The flames burned DeMona's arms, but she would not let go.

Redfeather watched as his grandson was pulled to certain death, and about to take two more souls with him. He was a firm believer that everyone lived for one defining moment in life and this was his. He turned to DeMona. "When I am gone, make sure they honor me in song."

"Wait!" DeMona tried to grab him with her free hand, but Redfeather had already leapt back through the rip and tackled Titus.

Now free of Titus's grip, Gabriel slingshotted forward through the rip, knocking DeMona and Rogue out through the other side. Ignoring the intense pain in his arm from the awkward way he had landed, Gabriel sprang to his feet and scrambled back toward the rip, which was shrinking faster by the second.

Gilgamesh held him back. "It's too late. You'll be cut in half if you try and pass back through the rip."

Gabriel struggled, eyes locked on the rip, which was now only slightly larger than a basketball. Through the portal, he saw his grandfather struggling with Titus futilely. The half-demon tossed the older man to the ground and raised his flaming sword.

"No!" Gabriel screamed, reaching for the shrinking tear.

Titus looked up, and for a second his and Gabriel's eyes met through the small hole. He gave Gabriel a nod that said it wasn't over before burying the flaming sword in Redfeather's chest. It was the last thing Gabriel saw before the rip snapped closed on a vision that would haunt him for the rest of his days.

• CHAPTER TEN •

After leaving the scrap yard, Asha made a brief stop at an apartment she kept on the Lower East Side of Manhattan. It was her safe house and not even Lisa and Lane knew about it. After a quick shower, she changed into fresh clothes, an outfit more befitting of her mood and her mission, steel toe combat boots, black leather pants, black leather jacket, and a black belly T-shirt that read BITCH in red letters.

Azuma was perched on the dresser, watching his mistress braid her dreadlocks into one plait that went down her back. He seemed agitated and with good reason. As familiar and witch, they were not only connected magically, but emotionally too. He walked across the dresser and nuzzled his furry face against her stomach in an attempt to comfort her.

Asha smiled and stroked the monkey's head. "Everything is going to be fine," she told him, wishing she was as confident as she sounded. It hurt Asha to kill her friend that night, but it hurt her more that Dutch had marked her as a traitor. Since she was a girl, she had looked at Dutch as somewhat of a father figure and was always loyal to him, but the assassination attempt told her that the loyalty was one-sided. She had two choices, wait around for one of Dutch's hit teams to succeed where Lisa and Lane had failed, or confront Dutch. Asha chose the latter. Armed with a few special items that she would need, Asha left the apartment and headed for the Triple Six.

The Triple Six night club was located in the Village, right off the West Side Highway in the shadow of where the WTC once stood. It wasn't the most well-advertised spot in town, but it was always packed to capacity with people trying to get in. To the world at large, it was one of the hottest underground clubs in the city, but to those in the know, it was where the wild things came to play. On any given night, you could find mortals and supernatural creatures partying side by side, with the humans being totally oblivious to the fact they had literally crossed the threshold of hell.

Before the taxi could come to a complete stop, Asha was already stepping out onto the curb with Azuma hot on her heels. The driver rolled down his window to demand his payment, thinking she was going to skip out on the fare. Asha tossed a wad of cash through the window and quieted him. It was way more money than the cost of the fare, so he was happy about the large tip the Black girl had given him. In a few blocks his happiness would turn to anger when the illusion spell she'd cast wore off, and he realized what he thought was money was actually napkins.

She skipped the line and marched straight to the entrance. When the man at the door spotted her, he whispered something into the small radio that connected the security team at the Triple Six. Asha knew she had blown the element of surprise, but was too pissed to care at that point. When he stepped in front of her to block her way, she had to look up at him because he stood easily a foot taller than her and outweighed her by nearly two hundred pounds. Though he was mortal, he was still dangerous.

"Stand aside, I'm here to see Dutch," Asha told him.

"Dutch ain't here, and you ain't welcome," the doorman said in a gravelly voice.

Asha clenched her fists. "I don't plan on repeating myself."

"Neither do I, so why don't you get the fuck—" That was as far as he got.

Asha delivered a blow to his throat that crushed his windpipe. Before his body hit the ground, she was inside the Triple Six.

It took her eyes a few seconds to adjust to the darkness sliced with flashing neon lights. She whispered softly into the monkey's ear and set him off to do her bidding, before slipping into the crowd. The place was so packed that the walls were sweating. People of all ages, races, and species drank and partied to the music blaring through the speakers. Asha was a regular, so there was little chance she would be able to move through the room without being recognized. She had to rely on speed where stealth had abandoned her. She was making progress when she saw two men in dark suits come from behind the black curtain and start searching faces in the crowd. One was human and the other a warlock, both in the service of Dutch.

Asha tried to detour through a mosh pit that was brewing near one of the main stages, but they'd spotted her. It was the warlock who reached her first, and he who caught the worst of it. He grabbed Asha's shoulder and opened his mouth to fire off a spell, when one of her bladed thumb rings made contact with the right side of his face. She flicked some of the excess blood onto the face of the human who had been with him and whispered the words of power. The human clawed at his face, trying to wipe away the blood splatter that was eating through his skin like acid, but it was useless. Without bothering to look back, she left both of them to die painfully on the dance floor.

She slipped behind the black curtain that separated the rest of the club from the upper level that was reserved for witches and warlocks. Standing at the top of the stairs was a dark-haired vampire named Angel who worked security for Dutch. He was whispering into the ear of a pretty young witch when he spotted Asha. Angel whispered something to the witch then shoved her through the door at the top of the stairs before turning his attention to Asha.

"How's it going, Asha?" Angel asked.

"I've been better," she said, making sure to keep a safe distance from him. At one time he and Asha had been good friends, but lately her friends had been trying to kill her, so she wasn't taking any chances.

"That's what I'm hearing. You know, I'd always heard rumors that you were suicidal but never paid much attention to them. Seeing you here knowing Dutch has put a price on your head makes me wonder."

Asha shrugged. "A wise man once said, if you can't find something to live for, you damn well better find something to die for."

Angel gave a nervous glance over his shoulder and spoke to Asha in a hushed tone. "Listen, Asha, you've always been nice to me. You never treated me like *the help*, which is more than I can say for some of these other snots of the Four Courts. I don't know what's going on between you and Dutch, and honestly I don't care as long as it doesn't put me in harm's way. The Black King wants to keep you quiet in the worst way, so if I were you, I'd get ghost."

"I need answers, Angel. Dutch has put me on a hit list, and I wanna know why," Asha told him.

"Asha, Dutch isn't even here. He left out of here sometime yesterday, and nobody has seen him since or knows where he is," Angel said honestly, hoping it would deter her.

"I'll bet I know someone who knows where he is. Is Falon inside?" Asha asked. He was a young warlock who Dutch had adopted into his circle, much like he did Asha. He was Dutch's eyes and ears as well as a toady.

"Yeah, he's here, but it doesn't matter. You know I can't let you in here, Asha. So why don't you just leave, and on my honor, I'll act as if I never saw you," Angel said sincerely.

Asha sighed. "In a perfect world, I would, but I think the two of us know how fucked up and far from perfect this world is, Angel."

Angel shook his head sadly. "And we both know that if I let you pass, then I'm as dead as you are when Dutch catches wind of it. I like you, Asha, but I'm not willing to die for you."

The vampire was so fast that by the time Asha had even realized he'd moved, he had already struck her twice across the jaw and sent her flying down the stairs. She bounced off a doorframe and back into his waiting arms. "You just had to make this hard, didn't you?" He grabbed her by the lapels of her leather jacket and propelled her into the ceiling, before letting her fall back down to the steps. "When I threw you the bone, you should've have taken it."

Asha was able to pull herself up along the wall and get back to her feet. She stood there on shaky legs, glaring down at Angel. "Bones are for dogs, and the only one I see still dangling on Dutch's leash is you." She leapt off the stairs and attacked Angel. She got in a few good licks, but she was no match for Angel's strength.

The enraged vampire slammed Asha's back into the wall with so much force that the plaster cracked. "You're stupid, kid. For as handy as you are with that magic, you're still mortal. I'm faster and stronger than you, so there's no way you can overpower me."

Asha looked Angel in the eyes, and suddenly she didn't appear as dazed as she had led him to believe. "I don't need to overpower you. I just need you to bleed," she said in a cold tone, before plunging her dagger into Angel's gut.

The vampire staggered, looking down curiously at the blade which was buried to the hilt in his stomach. With a grunt, he removed the knife and tossed it to the side. For a mortal, it would've been a critical blow, but not for a vampire. "Asha, all that little stunt did was piss me off."

"If that pissed you off, you're going to hate this. As with all things, the blood is the source. Now, vampire, let the blood you have stolen from your victims be your undoing. *Bleed!*" she shouted the command and put all of her will behind it. The wound in Angel's gut began to leak, but started to heal again. Asha had never tried using her blood magic on a vampire, so she had gambled it would work, and lost.

Angel moved lightning quick and pinned her against the wall with one hand. "At first I was gonna suck you dry and end it peacefully, but now I'm gonna make a mess of you first." He drew his fist back and swung.

"Stop!" Asha screamed and snapped her eyes closed, bracing for the blow that would surely crush her skull. To her surprise, a few seconds had gone by and she was still intact. When she opened her eyes, she saw Angel with his fist suspended in midair and a shocked expression on his face. From the way the veins were bulging in his neck, she could tell he was struggling, but he didn't seem to be able to move.

"What the hell have you done to me, witch?" Angel snarled.

Asha was too stunned to speak, because honestly she had no idea what she had done to Angel. It seemed that though she couldn't ignite the blood of a vampire as she could with things that were technically alive, her magic wasn't completely ineffective.

Asha had a theory that she wanted to test. "Release me," she said, forcing power into her words. Angel's hand opened, and Asha slid down against the wall, gasping. The vampire stared at her murderously, but couldn't move anything but his eyes. "Slap yourself, Angel." Reluctantly the vampire slapped himself across the face, proving Asha's theory correct. Though she may have not been able to make him bleed to death as she could with living things, she was still able to manipulate the blood, and because blood was what animated the living corpses, that meant she could control vampires. It was definitely an unexpected surprise.

"Cute, very cute, but you're still fucked. The minute you walk through that door, there'll be at least a dozen witches and warlocks on you trying to collect that bounty. You're good, but not even you can win against those odds."

Asha gave him a playful smile. "Then it's a good thing I'm not going in alone. Now, let's go have a chat with Falon."

• CHAPTER ELEVEN •

The Triple Six itself was in full swing with hundreds of people dancing, drugging, and raving, but in the VIP section, the mood was much more reserved. It too was normally packed with young witches and warlocks enjoying each other's company or huddled in the corners plotting in hushed tones, but that night it was somber. Since word had spread of the pending apocalypse, large numbers of supernatural communities had headed for higher ground to wait it out. Those who remained had either chosen a side or were waiting in the wings to pick over the scraps of whatever was left. Even Dutch had taken a mysterious leave of absence, which had stirred more than a few whispers, but none were foolish enough to speak of it within the walls of the Triple Six, especially with his eyes and ears, Falon, still lingering and watching from his favorite booth in the corner.

If Falon had to be described using just one word, it would've been *beautiful*. He was a fair-skinned young man with rich brown hair and amber eyes, with the faintest traces of a beard lining his smooth jaw. Dutch's young assistant sat in a dimly lit booth on the far side of the VIP section, shirtless under his white silk vest. His muscular arms rested around the shoulders of two pretty young men, who snuggled against him like cats. One was a blond and the other a brunette. The brunette held a joint pinched between his fingers, which Falon would lean forward to take a toke of every so often, and the blond would follow up by raising Falon's wine glass so that he might take a sip. Falon was the talk of all the witches of the Black Court for his striking good looks as well as his varying sexual tastes.

There was the sound of raised voices coming from near the entrance to the VIP section. Falon craned his neck to see what was going on, and his eyes almost popped out of his head when he saw the vampire Angel shoving his way through the crowd toward the booth, with a girl bound in chains. It was the traitor, Asha. Trailing him were three warlocks who served as members of the Hunt. The Hunt was the coven of witches' and warlocks' version of bounty hunters. Their automatic weapons were drawn in case the quarry attempted to escape. They all knew how dangerous Asha was, and nobody was willing to take any unnecessary chances.

"My, my, my, I must've been a good boy for Christmas to have come so early." Falon beamed. He shrugged the blond and the brunette away and gave Asha his undivided attention. "The mighty Asha, bound like a common criminal. I never thought I'd see the day."

"Enjoy it while you can, Falon. I don't plan to be here long," Asha told him.

"I'm sure you won't. As I'm told Dutch would prefer you

dead than alive, and I will take great pleasure in granting my king his wish, turncoat."

"That's bullshit, and you know it, Falon. None have been more loyal to this court than I. Dutch is framing me, and I wanna know why. Where is he?"

Falon shrugged. "Our king comes and goes as he pleases, and in his absence, I am the voice of the Black Court." He turned to Angel. "I heard she slaughtered two of our finest, Lisa and Lane. How did you manage to take her down?"

Angel's lips trembled, but he couldn't form words. Involuntarily his shoulders shrugged as if it were nothing.

"Funny, I never took you for the modest type." Falon scratched his stubble-covered chin.

"So, what was so important that Dutch dragged himself out of this cesspool?" Asha asked, drawing Falon's attention back to her. "I can count on one hand and probably still have fingers left as to the number of times he's left the Triple Six in the last few years."

"As I said, the king comes and goes as he pleases. It's no business of yours, traitor."

Asha laughed. "That speech may work with the novices, but you and I both know better than that. You know where Dutch is, and you're going to tell me willingly, or I'm going to drag the information out of you."

Now it was Falon's turn to laugh. "Even chained like a dog with no hope of escape, you sling your petty threats. Okay, I'll play your little game. I know exactly where Dutch is, but what in the Goddess's name makes you think I'll tell you? You are at my mercy."

"So it would seem, but one of the first lessons we learn in the novice circle is that nothing is ever what it seems." Asha rolled her shoulders, shrugging off the illusion spell she had cast before she came in, and the chains vanished. "Or have you been suckling at your master's cock so long that you've forgotten?"

"Angel, restrain her!" Falon commanded. Angel stood there as immobile as he had been in the hall. "Didn't you hear me? Do something, vampire!"

Asha looked over her shoulder at Angel. "You heard him. Do something, vampire."

This time Angel did move. He turned to the warlock closest to him and put his fist through his chest, ripping out his heart and throwing the still beating muscle on the table. Falon sat in utter shock watching the heart pump blood onto the black tablecloth. Falon shot to his feet and pointed his finger accusingly. "Treason," he hissed.

"Not treason, magic . . . *blood* magic." Asha cackled. "Kill them all, but bring Falon to me," she commanded.

Like a robot, Angel stumbled forward to do his mistress's bidding. The remaining two warlocks who had followed him in leapt onto his back in an attempt to restrain him and keep him from getting to Falon, but their physical strength was no match for that of the vampire. Angel tore them to shreds with very little effort and turned to attack Falon, but was instead intercepted by the young blond and brunette. The brunette slipped behind Angel, producing a length of silver chain that he looped around the vampire's neck, which burned his skin and slowed him but didn't stop him. While Angel struggled with the brunette, the blond broke off a piece of the wooden table and plunged it into Angel's heart. The vampire collapsed into a pile of ash, leaving Asha on her own.

Falon smirked, knowing he had her trapped. "Bring me the bitch's head."

The blond and brunette crisscrossed each other, moving

on Asha and throwing a series of complex blows. They had to have been working together for years to move with that kind of precision, same as it had been with Lisa and Lane. For them to be so young, she had to admit they were good, but she was better.

The brunette conjured a spell and tried to lay hands on Asha to infect her with it, but she grabbed his arm and his palm found the blond's face. The skin on his cheek began to crackle, and he fell to the ground, foaming from the mouth. Asha twisted her body and broke the brunette's arm before throwing him through the glass bar. When she turned her attention back to Falon, he was gone.

She looked around the room and spotted him just as he disappeared through the looking glass on the back wall. Asha strode up to the mirror that served as the entrance into Dutch's private chamber. The looking glass was protected by a spell that would shred anyone who tried to pass without knowing the proper incantation, but who needed spells when you had rage. Asha channeled her anger, throwing her hands and will forward, and the mirror imploded.

Falon fumbled with the panel built into Dutch's drawer and came up holding a handgun. Before he could point it, let alone use it, Asha had bounded over the desk and kicked him hard in the chest, sending him spilling into the plush leather chair. He tried again for the gun, and lost his hand to the black dagger. Blood squirted from Falon's stump all over Dutch's antique wooden desk.

"My hand!" Falon wailed.

Asha snatched him from the chair by the front of his vest. "It'll be your life if you don't tell me where Dutch has gone and why he wants me dead."

"I don't know!" Falon exclaimed.

"Wrong answer." Asha snapped her hand closed, and Falon began to bleed heavier. "You better sing me a song or they're gonna have to send a lifeboat in here to fish you from a river of your own blood."

Falon composed himself as best he could. "Asha, on my mother's eyes, I don't know why Dutch wants you dead. All he's told any of us is that you were on some kind of power trip. He says that you cut a deal with the dark lord to overthrow the ruling bodies of the courts of witches and warlocks."

Asha jerked her fist upward, and blood squirted up from Falon's hand. "Bullshit! Since I was a kid I've pledged my life to the Black Court and that piece of shit Dutch. Why would I try to cross him?"

"Asha, don't shoot the messenger. You wanted straight talk, and I gave it to you. Now please stop this bleeding; I'm getting dizzy."

"I ain't done with you, pretty boy. Where is Dutch?"

Falon shook his head from side to side. "Asha, you know I can't—"

She didn't even let him finish. Asha waved her hands in a pattern and pulled back like the reins on a horse, forcing more blood from the stump. "You'll run out of blood long before I get tired," Asha told him.

Falon held his good hand up in surrender. "Dutch is in upstate New York at a place called Raven Wood."

Asha was taken back by this. Dutch rarely left the Triple Six, let alone traveled outside New York City. "What's going on at Raven Wood that's pulled that king cobra out of its den?"

"I don't know," Falon said, hoping she believed him. She didn't. Asha whipped her hands again and pulled a stream of blood from Falon's nose. "Okay, okay. All I know is that there's some kind of important conference going on at Raven Wood. Dutch never said what it was about and insisted on going by himself. I swear that's all I know. Please make it stop." He was in tears.

Asha stared at Falon in disgust. If people like Falon would be left to rule the Black Court once the elders moved on, then she was happy to be making a clean break from it. "Okay, we're done, Falon."

Falon clutched his bloody stump to his chest. "Thank the Goddess. Asha, we've never been the best of friends, but you understand the position the information I've given you will put me in if anyone finds out. Promise it'll stay between us."

"Falon, neither the tale of your act of cowardice or *you* will ever leave this room. You have my word on that." Asha clapped her hands together, and Falon's body exploded like a water balloon, coating everything in the office with blood, including the oil painting of Dutch and the White Queen that hung on the wall behind the desk.

Asha looked up at the painting. "I wonder how Dutch will feel about the changes I've made to his décor." She laughed to herself.

Asha was about to leave when something about the painting caught her eye. The blood was eating away at the paint and revealed something hidden behind the image. She wiped her hand across the bottom of the picture until the paint rubbed away and she could make out words that looked like they'd been etched into the canvas itself. She couldn't read them, but she knew someone who might be able to. Carefully, she cut the painting from the frame and rolled it up to take with her.

Asha's exit from the Triple Six went far smoother than her entrance. What was left of the security team was standing outside the VIP section when she descended the stairs, but none dared to make a move on her after what she had just done to Falon and the others. They simply watched her to make sure she left without causing any more damage. When she got to the exit, Azuma came scuttling through the crowd and jumped on her shoulder. He squawked something into her ear and dropped a small parcel in her hand. "Good work," she told him before stuffing it into her pocket. She then turned around and addressed the crowd that was watching her nervously. "When Dutch comes out of hiding, be sure to tell him that Asha was the one who did this." And with that, she left.

· CHAPTER TWELVE ·

Back at the scrap yard, the mood was sullen. A handful of mortals and supernatural beings had done the impossible. Not only had they escaped the Iron Mountains, but they had slain the prince of the goblins and crippled Titus's army in the process. It should've been a joyous moment, but it wasn't. Their victory had come with a very heavy price tag.

Gilgamesh hadn't said much to anyone since they had come through the rip. Teko had not only been an invaluable part of his organization, but a dear friend, and now he was dead. They'd offered to hold a vigil for him, but Gilgamesh had declined, instead opting to honor him in private. Rogue was about to offer to go with him, but the dark elf had already disappeared into the shadows of the scrap yard. Whether he would return or not to continue aiding in their cause was anyone's guess, but whatever he decided, no one could blame him. Had it not been for Gilgamesh and Teko, they'd have never made it in or out of the Iron Mountains.

Morgan was there to greet the travelers, helping them get their wounded below to what served as the compound's makeshift infirmary. It was really a large storage room which Jonas had equipped with cots and high-tech medical equipment. Jackson lay on one cot, engaged in a conversation with Lydia. He was still in a great deal of pain, but was fast on the road to recovery, which had been the topic of debate at the compound. It was no secret that years prior he had suffered a vampire attack, and though the bites didn't turn him, they did affect his anatomy. Since the attack, they had found that Jackson could heal faster than a normal human, but he had never had a wound of that magnitude before. The fact that he was almost fully recovered in less than twenty-four hours made some wonder, especially Finnious.

The little wraith had tried to heal Jackson and was making progress when he felt the presence. It was as if there were two people inhabiting Jackson's soul, but no sooner had he felt it than the presence was gone again. It frightened him so bad that he hadn't come within five feet of Jackson since they'd come back inside the compound. He quietly sat in a chair in the corner, listening to Jackson and Lydia talk while wondering exactly what Jackson was. Everyone else seemed to think he was a human who had simply been lucky enough to survive a vampire bite, but Finnious didn't.

When Finnious saw Rogue and the others enter the room, he perked up, but his mood changed when he saw Morgan carrying Lucy's prone body. Her skin was pail and the stench of death hung so strong on her that it burned the wraith's nose. "What's wrong with her?"

"Poisoned." Cristobel entered the room, followed by Mavis.

The two dwarves got stares from those who had never seen their kind, but did not take offense.

Finnious watched curiously as Morgan gently placed Lucy on the cot in the center of the room that Jonas used as his examining table. The bulky halogen light that hung from a crane at the head of the bed shone brightly on her pale yet still beautiful face. Finnious's hands gripped the edges of the table while he watched Jonas start to undo Lucy's blouse to take her vitals.

"Finnious, maybe you should step out of the room while we work so as not to be in the way," Jonas suggested.

"Maybe I can help," Finnious offered.

"Kid, you're aces with those magic hands of yours on flesh wounds, but we all saw what happened the last time somebody was poisoned," Jackson said from a sitting position on his cot. "Take a powder." He nodded toward the door.

Finnious folded his arms and glared at Jackson challengingly. It was Lydia who defused it by taking him by the hand. "Come on, let's raid the pantry and see if we can rustle up some food. I'm sure everyone is hungry." She led Finnious toward the door. Before he left, he shot Jackson a dirty look over his shoulder.

In the hallway they passed DeMona and another Valkrin whom they had never seen. DeMona made the introductions and gave Lydia the short version of their adventure. Finnious only half listened as his attention was on the pink-haired girl who walked between the two warrior women. He had never met another of the fey, but somehow he instinctively knew she was some sort of sprite or fairy.

Leah must've felt him staring because she turned her molten gold eyes on him. The glow that surrounded Finnious was invisible to mortal eyes, but Leah could see it quite clearly. Her head cocked to one side as she tried to figure out what to make of the pale young man in the oversized sweatshirt, and if necessary, how she could use him to her advantage when the time came.

When Gabriel entered the infirmary, there was an uncomfortable silence as if they had been talking about something before he came in that they didn't want him to hear. He didn't need a crystal ball to know what they were all thinking. They had followed him into the depths of hell, and when the time came for him to live up to the hype, he had failed them all, including himself.

When they'd arrived, Jonas wanted an immediate debriefing as to the events that had transpired under the mountains, but Gabriel was still in a state of shock, so he had to get the account from the others while he attended Gabriel's broken arm. Jonas had put it in a makeshift splint and urged him to get some rest, but there was no way he could sleep. Every time he closed his eyes, he saw the death of his grandfather. He replayed the scene over in his head a million times and tried to figure out what he could've done differently and to produce an alternative outcome, but he couldn't. The sad fact was that the only way for them to escape the Iron Mountains was for a Redfeather to die, and part of him wished it had been him instead of his grandfather.

Lucy lay on a cot in the center of the room. Mavis wiped the girl's forehead with a cool rag, trying to keep the fever down while Jonas examined her with his machines. Mercy and Cristobel looked on curiously while they worked. Jonas was a man versed in a great many things, but he looked stumped.

Defeat was etched heavy across his face, and Gabriel knew exactly how he was feeling.

Gabriel pulled out the trident and held it in his hands, studying it. He could still fill the magic that dwelled in it, but not the connection. It was as if when Titus broke his arm, he had also broken his will, and the Nimrod knew it. "Where the hell were you when I needed you?"

"Instruments of magic are only as strong as the will of those who wield them." Leah's voice startled Gabriel. He didn't even hear her approach. She was speaking to him, but her eyes were on the Nimrod.

"What do you know about magic when you're just a kid?" Gabriel asked.

Leah smiled. "Don't let my appearance fool you. I am a child of magic, as are all fey."

Gabriel laughed. "You're right. Sorry, I keep forgetting you're not human."

Leah sat on the stool next to him. "None of us really are, contrary to what some believe. All species are descendants of magical things, but time has thinned the blood and erased the memories of when there was only one world: Midland." Her voice sounded far away.

"You speak of it as if you remember," Gabriel said.

Leah caught herself. "Of course I don't. Even though I'm a fey, I'm still only a child, right?" She gave him an enchanting smile. "So, how did you come into possession of it?" She nodded at the fork.

"I guess you might say it fell into my lap." Gabriel cut his eyes at DeMona. "Ever since then, it's brought nothing but to misery to my life."

"With great power comes great responsibility," Leah said.

"Yeah, maybe more responsibility than I was ready to handle."

"The Goddess sometimes tests us by bringing things or situations into our lives, but never does she give us more than what we are able to handle. However, you have to want to. Why do you think the Nimrod no longer responds to you?"

The question took Gabriel by surprise because he hadn't told anyone about the broken connection. "Maybe because it knows I'm too weak to control it. I mean, look at me." He motioned toward his bruised frame.

Leah laughed, and when she did, it made Gabriel think of Christmas bells. "Physical strength means nothing when dealing with things like the Nimrod. It is only as strong as the will of he who commands it. When Titus broke your body, he also broke your will, and this is why the Nimrod will no longer answer your call."

Gabriel weighed her words. Leah was right. When he had slain the Stalkers and battled the demon Riel, he was afraid but still confident that he had a chance. With Titus, he felt no such confidence. From the first time he felt the half-demon's power, he allowed doubt to creep into his heart. Even with the Nimrod, he wasn't sure if he could beat him, and that's why he failed.

Gabriel looked at the Nimrod. He could still feel the prickles of power, so he knew it was in there, he just had to pull himself together enough to drag it out. "You know, for a kid, you make a lot of sense."

Leah gave him her warmest smile. They sat there in silence for a few seconds, with Leah's eyes involuntarily going to the Nimrod. Finally she asked, "May I see it?"

Gabriel was hesitant. "I don't know. This thing is pretty dangerous."

"Doesn't look very dangerous; it just looks broken to me. You know, I've been around magic all my life, and my father was a weaponsmith. Maybe I can help you figure out what's wrong with it." She stuck her hand out.

"Leah, this isn't a toy," Gabriel told her, but he made no attempt to move it out of her reach. He knew that he shouldn't let the girl touch the Nimrod because there was no way to tell how it would react, but when he looked down into her golden eyes, his heart melted. Not letting her hold the Nimrod would make her sad, and Gabriel couldn't bear to see Leah sad. He was just about to put the broken fork in her hand, when Rogue came through the door and snapped him out of it.

"You okay, kid?" Rogue slapped him on the back.

"Yeah, I'm okay." Gabriel stuffed the fork back into his pants. "My arm just hurts like hell."

"Maybe Jonas has some aspirin or something. I'll find out for you, kid." He patted Gabriel on the shoulder. He and Leah made brief eye contact, but neither lingered. It was just long enough for one to let the other know they were both watching each other. "What's the prognosis, doc?" he asked Jonas.

The Medusan shook his head sadly. "I have to admit, I'm stumped. I've never dealt with Slov venom firsthand, but from the stories I've read, it's almost always fatal if not treated immediately, and the gods only know how long it's had to do its work on her."

"Is there nothing we can do?" Gabriel asked.

"I'm a scientist, not a magician or a healer, so my hands are tied, Gabriel. Possibly if we had one of the coven's healers, they could do something, but even if we were to contact them, I fear she'll be dead before they can get here."

"Well, I don't know if she's a healer, but a witch just walked through the front door." Jackson nodded to one of the video monitors. Asha had just entered the scrap yard and was making hurried steps toward the compound.

"I'll shut off the security system, so she can pass without incident." Jonas rolled his sleeve back and tapped in a code on what looked like a digital wristwatch. "Would one of you mind going upstairs to bring her to the infirmary?"

"I'll do it," DeMona volunteered.

When DeMona left the room, Jonas turned his attention back to Lucy. "Maybe Asha knows something that we don't. At the very least, I'm glad she's here to say her goodbyes to a sister witch."

"They didn't exactly get along," Gabriel said, which seemed to draw him a look from Rogue. He hadn't meant it to sound like that.

"Still, they had history," Rogue told him.

Mavis shook her head sadly. She was trying not to cry, but her eyes were misty. "It always saddens me to see those so young pass on. Poor child." Leah walked up next to Mavis and took her hand. Her touch seemed to soothe her.

"Nobody is dying. We're not giving up until she stops breathing. Everybody understand?" Rogue said a little harsher than he had meant to. Through his shadow eyes, Rogue could see Lucy's light dimming, and in his heart he knew there wasn't anything they could do for her. He was no stranger to death, but he had nieces that were about Lucy's age, so watching her die was tough for him.

"Might I give her a kiss?" Leah asked, drawing curious glances from everyone. "They say that a kiss of the fey is supposed to bring luck, so maybe it'll help." She looked around at them innocently.

"Fine." Rogue stepped to the side so Leah could get to the table.

Leah walked to Lucy's bedside and ran her dainty fingers up her arm. She could still feel the pinpricks of Lucy's magic, but her lifeforce was almost nonexistent. She was leaning in to place a soft kiss on Lucy's lips when Asha and DeMona walked in.

"Guys, I've got something to show you and—" Asha began, but her words were cut off when she saw Leah hovering over Lucy. Unlike the rest of them, she could see what hid within the shell of the little girl. "Get away from her." Asha flicked out two of her bladed disks.

DeMona jumped in the way and the disks bounced off her and buried themselves in the wall next to Gabriel's head. She grabbed Asha by the throat and lifted her off her feet. "What are you, some kind of sicko? That's a kid, Asha!" DeMona snarled.

"That ain't no kid. Look at her," Asha croaked.

All eyes turned to Leah, and for the first time, they saw it. There was a ghostly figure clinging to the little girl. They couldn't be sure what it was, but it radiated power. "Too late," Leah said, her voice thick with power.

"The hell it is." Morgan went to reach for Leah and found that he couldn't move, and neither could anyone else in the room. Leah had cast some type of spell on them.

"Silly mortals, instead of trying to stop me, you should be thanking me." Leah laughed. She leaned in, and the moment her lips touched Lucy's, the room was filled with brilliant white light.

• CHAPTER THIRTEEN •

Hearing the commotion in the infirmary brought Lydia and Finnious running. Lydia was first through the door, Spear of Truth at the ready. Finnious was closely behind her, holding a small knife in his trembling hands. Before he had even stepped into the room, he could feel the wild magic running through it. All but one person was frozen as stiff as statues. When Finnious looked to the source of the spell, he dropped his blade and gasped.

"What's going on, Fin?" Lydia asked when she heard the blade hit the floor.

He tried to speak, but was too stunned.

The child Leah was sprawled out on the floor and unconscious. The magic from whatever spell had been used against her crackled around her body. Standing over her was Lucy, or at least he thought so at first glance. He couldn't understand how she had been on the brink of death a few minutes prior, but was now not only up and around, but her aura was ten times stronger than it had been. Her dark hair floated on a phantom wind, and she turned to look at Finnious. When he saw the molten gold eyes starting at him, he knew that it was Lucy's body, but not her spirit that inhabited it.

"Hello, children," spoke Leah's spirit. The force of her words produced a wind that swept through the room.

Following the sound, Lydia raised the spear. "I don't know who you are or what you are or why you're here, but know that to do anything, you'll have to go through me."

Leah walked slowly toward the youngsters. Lydia struck with the spear, but Leah plucked it from her hand and gave it a comical look before tossing it to the side. "No weapon forged by man or other can harm the Goddess." She touched her finger to Lydia's forehead and rendered her immobile like the others, then turned her attention to Finnious.

Finnious called the light to his hands and held them up. "Stay back! I won't let you hurt my friends."

Leah smirked. "Trust me, if I had intentions on killing you or your friends, there would be little you could do to prevent it, wraith. Great power dwells within you, but you are too new to your gifts and too afraid to try and understand them, to challenge me. Your ignorance is the only reason I take no offense in you even thinking to threaten the Goddess." She looked over her new young and taut arms. "She will do nicely." She turned back to Finnious. "For more years than I care to remember, I was a prisoner of the dark lord, condemned to leapfrog from child to child, never again to know what it is to walk on the clouds, or be touched by a man. I am captive no more, and the sacrifice of your friends made it so." She looked out at the room full of frozen faces. Her eyes stopped and lingered on Gabriel. "A debt is owed." She moved to

Gabriel and laid her hands on his broken arm. "So a debt will be paid. Faith is the key to victory," Leah whispered into Gabriel's ear before stepping back. "The scales are now balanced between us." She spread her arms and called her power.

"Wait, why did you kill Lucy?" Finnious blurted out. He wasn't really sure why he asked the question, but he wanted to be able to at least tell her family why she died.

Leah looked over her shoulder at the vacant cot then turned back to Finnious. Her eyes were sad. "I did not kill Lucy; I released her from her suffering, and in doing so, I freed myself." Without another word, she vanished.

Not long after Leah had vanished, everyone began to stir again. Even though they had been frozen, they had been able to see and hear the exchange between Leah and Finnious. Their moods ranged from shock to anger to embarrassment.

DeMona took her hands from around Asha's throat and lowered her head in embarrassment. She had been manipulated by the child and almost killed an ally because of it. "Asha, I don't know what . . ."

"It's nothing." Asha rubbed her sore neck. "She enthralled you; any of us could've fallen victim to one as strong as her."

"How did you know she was masquerading?" Jonas asked.

Asha shrugged. "I don't know. It's like when I came in here and saw her, something just didn't look right. Call it witch's intuition."

"Well, she's lucky she left when she did." Jackson was on his feet, but his legs didn't look steady. "Had I been able to move . . ." He staggered to one side and was about to topple over, but Asha caught him and helped guide him to a sitting position on one of the cots.

"If that was who I think it was, then there wouldn't have been much you or any of us could've done. She could've squashed us like ants," Asha told him.

"She called herself the Goddess. Was she?" Finnious asked.

"Yes and no," Asha said. "Among us, the Goddess was the original source of all things, but in some lore, they say she had sisters, one being called Leah, the Goddess of Truth."

"I've heard of her," Rogue chimed in. "She's supposed to be a real piece of work. If that was *the* Leah, then we should all consider ourselves lucky."

There was a low moan across the room. They all turned to see the little girl on the floor stirring. DeMona moved in, claws extended and ready to strike. She had been played by magic once tonight and didn't intend on it happening again. She reached down and grabbed the girl by her soiled night-gown, flipping her over. Terrified and confused brown eyes stared up at the Valkrin.

"Don't hurt me," the terrified girl pleaded.

DeMona ignored her pleas and snatched her to her feet. "You won't fool me twice, Leah."

The girl looked even more confused than she had before. "Who is Leah? My name is Lucy."

It seemed like the longer the night wore on, the stranger it got. The little girl DeMona had almost killed now sat on the ex-amining table, looking at them all curiously while Jonas checked her vitals. He had to use a stethoscope because noth-ing that ran on electricity seemed to work with the girl. She was giving off some kind of energy that was shorting out his equipment.

When she woke up claiming to be Lucy, they'd all thought it was another trick by the Goddess Leah, so they were cautious. She was Lucy in spirit and name, but that's where it ended. Her mind was almost a completely clean slate, with her only knowing her name and the fact that she was a witch. Everything else that had been Lucy was gone. Asha and Finnious both looked her over and confirmed her story. The presence of the Goddess was gone, and the girl was indeed what she appeared to be, a prepubescent witch. The Goddess didn't kill her, after all; she only swapped bodies, taking the poisoned, ravaged adult as her own and leaving behind a healthy child.

"So, she didn't lie," Finnious said in amazement.

"What do you mean, Fin?" Rogue asked.

"The Goddess told me that she didn't kill Lucy, only released her from her suffering," Finnious explained.

"Considering that I can find no traces of the poison, I would say that she indeed kept her word," Jonas said.

Asha noticed the new Lucy staring at her so she stared back. She and Lucy had been bitter rivals for years, and she wondered if that part of her had carried over with the rest of her. To her surprise, the girl got up off the table and walked over to her. She pushed her pale pink hair from her face and looked up at Asha quizzically.

"I know you, don't I?" Lucy asked.

"Yes, we know each other very well."

Lucy smiled and hugged Asha's waist, catching her totally off guard. "I knew it!" She looked up at Asha with joy in her eyes. "When I saw you staring at me, I knew we were the same. You're a witch too! Are we related in some way?" she asked innocently.

Asha was stumped for a moment. Finally she nodded. "We are now, kid."

"I hate to break up your little moment, but what were you gonna show us when you busted in here?" Jackson asked. He gave Asha a hard time whenever he could.

Asha cut her eyes at him and ignored his attitude, instead handing Jonas the painting she had taken from Dutch's office. Jonas carefully unrolled it on the examining table and adjusted the overhead light. It was a picture of Dutch and the White Queen that was painted on a material that he had never seen.

"What am I looking at?" Jonas asked Asha.

"I was hoping you could tell me." Asha sliced open her hand and let blood drop onto the parchment. As the blood soaked in, something became visible behind the picture. It was a diagram for a powerful spell, but the instructions were written in a tongue she didn't recognize.

Jonas looked over the parchment for a while, carefully touching certain areas and annunciating words. "This is old, very old. I can make out parts of it, but I would need time to study it before I could translate correctly."

"I don't know about the language, but the diagram itself looks vaguely familiar to me. It's like I've seen it somewhere," Rogue said, wracking his brain.

"You've been seeing it all your life, but you were too concerned with chasing tail to pay attention." Gilgamesh stepped from the shadows of the infirmary. No one was quite sure how he'd gotten past Jonas's high-tech security system to get in undetected. "That's the Devil's Trap."

Rogue looked at the diagram again before turning back to the elf. "Mesh, I've seen the Devil's Trap cast before, and that ain't it."

Gilgamesh laughed at Rogue's protest. "What you saw were weak offshoots, parlor tricks by the death mongers to control stray spirits. This"—he tapped his finger on the parchment—"could hold damn near anything, and make it play nice."

"What would Dutch need with a spirit trap?" Asha asked. She knew Dutch had been known to dabble in the dark arts, but never death magic.

"He doesn't, but Titus does. The Rising ceremony requires several things, most importantly host bodies and spirits to inhabit them," Gilgamesh explained.

"The First Guard were men and women of God, their ghosts would never serve evil willingly," Jonas challenged.

"Yes, but the Devil's Trap won't leave them a choice," Gilgamesh told him. "Titus is a tyrant, and those who refuse to serve him willingly will serve him by force."

"So if Titus has got everything all mapped out, why does he need the Nimrod?" DeMona asked.

Gilgamesh shot Gabriel a look that said the answer was obvious. "Haven't you been paying attention to why the dark order has been putting so much energy into killing you? The First Guard will lead Titus's earthly army, but first he has to get the army here; and to get that many demons to this side of the playing field in one shot, he's gonna need to create a *very* huge rip in the veil."

"He means to call the Dark Storm," Rogue said as the tumblers fell into place.

Gilgamesh winked. "Bingo. He plans to use the Nimrod to bust the veil wide open and usher in the forces of hell from the other side."

"Over my dead body!" Gabriel said.

"I think that's the general idea," Gilgamesh countered. "If we don't stop him, then this world and everyone in it is lost."

"Thought you didn't care what happened to the humans?" Rogue asked.

"I don't. Humans are barbaric, and even if Titus fails, they'll probably wipe each other out over time. But for as much as I hate to admit it, the fates of our two worlds are intertwined. If this realm is conquered, the Midland will surely be next, and I'll not see the Black Forest burned or my people enslaved."

Asha shook her head. "If I wasn't sure before, I'm absolutely sure now: I hate your arrogant ass."

Gilgamesh snorted. "How you feel about me is of little concern, blood witch. What's important is that we need each other to save our respective worlds."

"So what do we do now, sit around and wait for another attack?" Morgan asked.

"No, we take the fight to Titus. No more running. We go on the offense and hit them at Raven Wood," Gabriel said.

"I'm with you on that, Gabriel, but it'll take us hours to drive upstate to Raven Wood, and by then, Titus may have already completed the Rising," DeMona pointed out.

"Then instead of taking the local route, we take the express." Rogue laid Teko's blade on the table.

"What good will the sword do us when its master is dead and with him the power to open rips?" Mercy asked.

"Yes, Teko is dead, but not the magic. When I used my shadow magic to snag it before the rip closed, the collective made contact and I discovered its secret. Teko wielded it valiantly, but I think it was originally crafted to serve another." Rogue cut his eyes at Gilgamesh. "Am I right?"

"Nicely done, detective." Gilgamesh smiled. He picked the blade up, and it began to glow bright. "My father had the sword made for me when I reached puberty and showed signs that I had a deeper connection with the magic of the Black Forest than any of my kinsmen, but I have never had the patience for magic. I am a soldier and had no time to be bothered with learning spell casting, so I taught another the blade's secrets. Teko's ability surpassed my father's greatest expectations of me, which is why my father always treated Teko like the son he'd never had," he said almost shamefully.

Rogue placed a hand on Gilgamesh's shoulder. "You may not have grown into the man that your father wanted you to be, but you did grow into the man you needed to be."

"Okay, so then why don't you fire that thing up, and let's get to Raven Wood and kick some demon ass," Asha said. She then saw a look of uncertainty cross Gilgamesh's face. "You do know how to use it, don't you?"

"Yes, I am familiar with how to use it, but as I said, it was Teko who learned to master my father's gift to me. I can open a rip aimed at Raven Wood, but I cannot say for sure that I will have the accuracy that Teko did," Gilgamesh admitted.

"Then get us as close as you can, and we'll sort the rest out when we get there," Rogue told him.

"A less than sound plan, but I am willing to fight alongside you. My question is: How do we destroy the Devil's Trap?" Mercy asked. It was a good question.

Jonas spoke up. "I think I may have an answer to that." He had been studying the diagram the whole time. "The Devil's Trap requires a large amount of power, but the power must be distributed evenly. If we upset the balance, then we may be able to short-circuit it."

"I get it, like overcharging a car battery." Gabriel caught

on to Jonas's line of thinking. "But where are we gonna get that kind of power?" When all eyes turned to him, he understood the plan, but couldn't say that it sat easy with him.

"You think you're up to it, kid?" Rogue asked.

Gabriel looked at the Nimrod, which was still quiet. "I guess we'll find out soon, won't we?"

• CHAPTER FOURTEEN •

When Titus returned to Raven Wood, he was in foul mood. The mission that he had *personally* led to stop the invaders at the Iron Mountains was an utter failure. He'd had the Nimrod literally in his hands and couldn't hold onto it. Not only had Gabriel and his friends escaped, but they'd crippled his army and his plans.

With Orden dead and the goblins without a leader, the horde was thrown into total disarray. Democracy had never been something goblins embraced; instead, the right of succession was decided by steel and blood. A civil war had broken out with one side trying to eradicate the other for control of the Iron Throne. Until they selected another leader, they would be little good to Titus or his cause.

Then there was Leah. Losing possession of the Goddess of Truth was something Titus hadn't planned on in all this. Free from her prison, the Goddess's power could no longer be suppressed, and she was free to take an adult host to speed her recovery. Still, it would be a minute before she was fully restored. However, when she was, she would surely come looking for Titus to repay him for his years of cruelty. They could no longer afford to wait; the Rising would have to commence immediately. He just hoped that all was ready.

The first person he saw when he returned to Raven Wood was Flagg, his personal assistant and resident spell caster. The mage was dressed in a shirt and tie under a vest, and slacks. He was smiling until he saw Titus's tattered clothing and the grim expression on his face.

"I take it all didn't go well with your trip," Flagg said.

"And I take it you have a knack for stating the obvious," Titus grumbled.

He walked past the mage and continued on to the room he had designated as his personal study. When he didn't close the door behind him, Flagg took it as an invitation and followed.

Titus flopped on one of the couches wearily and exhaled deeply. "The goblin prince has fallen, and Leah has managed to escape with the human and his bunch."

Flagg was relieved to hear that Orden was dead because the goblin prince terrified him, but the news of Leah's escape unnerved him. He had warned Titus time and again about keeping the Goddess alive instead of destroying her while she was vulnerable, but he wouldn't listen, and as a result, they now had a very powerful enemy loose somewhere in the world.

"Shall I dispatch Riel and his Stalkers to retrieve her?" Flagg asked.

"Don't bother. We have no way to know how much of her power she's recovered by now, and sending men after her could be sending lambs to the slaughter. We need all the bodies available to us to fortify Raven Wood for the ceremony."

"But the Goddess—"

Titus cut him off. "Will bow like the rest once my army of darkness marches across this world." He walked over to the window and looked out at the front yard. His eyes were fixed on something in the darkness. "I have not come this far to be thwarted," he said with conviction to his voice.

Flagg had served Titus long enough to know not to press the issue further. "Of course, Lord Titus. On to more pressing business. The Devil's Trap is set. I took the liberty of having one of my minions scout an alternate power source just in case things didn't go according to plan. It took some doing, but the relic he's secured should do nicely. He should reach us by morning, and we can begin the Rising as soon as tomorrow at sundown."

"We will perform the Rising tonight," Titus informed him, surprising the mage.

"With all due respect, my lord, I think it's too soon. The Rising is no easy task, and our spell casters are exhausted from preparing these last few days. Aside from that, the Devil's Trap will require a great deal of power, power which we don't have access to yet."

"We've got all the power we need." Titus motioned for Flagg to look out the window.

Flagg peered down to the courtyard, and his eyes widened in shock. Marching across the front lawn were at least two dozen corpses, in all stages of decay. Leading them like the Pied Piper was Riel. "You mean to power it with them?"

"What is more powerful than the human soul?"

Flagg shook his head. "It's too risky. Whatever spirits that still cling to those corpses will be weak and displaced. Even if we feed all Riel's puppets to the Trap, it still may not be enough to power it."

"If the spirits clinging to those corpses aren't enough to power it, then I'll have to find slightly fresher ones to power it." Titus gave Flagg a look that made him uneasy.

"As you command." Flagg half bowed. "I'll have the warlock make ready."

Less than an hour later, Titus came out of the study dressed in black pants and a black shirt that was unbuttoned at the collar. Looking closely one could see the raised pink welt on his chest, where the point of the Nimrod still rested. As he crossed the living room, Helena fell in step beside him, carrying a sleek black case. The two of them walked in silence to the door that led to the basement. Titus laid his hand on the knob and whispered the words of power while turning the knob counterclockwise three times before opening the door. Had he not, it would've simply opened up to a furnished basement instead of a dark and musty stairwell that led to a level of the house that wasn't on the original blueprint.

As they descended the stairs, the air became thicker and more humid. Those sensitive enough to it could feel the powerful magic coming up long before they exited the stairwell and stepped out into a receiving area. The corpses that had been marched in stood around dumbstruck, while young girls dressed in crimson robes prepared them for what was to come. Leaning against the wall was the war demon Riel.

"Greetings, oh great and powerful Titus." He bowed dramatically. "I, your most humble servant, greet you with—"

"Enough with your ego stroking, demon." Titus waved him off. "Will these corpses hold up to what is required of them?"

"You mean, stand up to watching their bodies burned to ash while what little soul they have left in them is sucked into your war machine?" Riel shrugged. "I don't see why not. I know you requested those who are slightly more recently departed, and thanks to your little bloodhound, I was able to do just that."

Titus smiled. "Ah yes, and where is she now?"

"Inside with the rest of the stiffs and soon-to-be stiffs." Riel nodded toward a door at the end of the hall.

"Then let's not keep her waiting too long." Titus led the way to the door.

Standing on either side of the thick iron door were two beefy young men with automatic weapons slung over their shoulders. At a glance, they appeared human, but their white eyes gave them away. Their shells were those of humans, but the souls that dwelled within them were demons in service to Riel. The two guards nodded and stepped to the side, opening the door for the trio.

Riel had learned from experience never to be the first one to enter a room when he wasn't sure what he was walking into, so he let Titus and Helena go in first. The inside of the room looked almost like the inside of an antique clock with its massive gears. There were twelve sarcophagi forming a circle around the room, each sitting on pentagrams that were drawn in human blood. Moving around the room, double-checking everything, was the warlock Dutch.

Dutch was a ruggedly handsome man with dark and curly hair that stopped just above his shoulder. For nearly a century, he had served as the King of the Black Court of Witches and Warlocks. He was arguably the most powerful warlock in all the courts, but his greed drove him to want more. In exchange for his services, Titus had promised to elevate him from King of the Black Court to the King of All Spell Casters. Of course, it would mean enslaving those whom he pledged to protect, but the offer was too good for Dutch to pass up. When he turned around and noticed Titus, he moved to greet him.

"Greetings, Lord Titus, and welcome to the Devil's Trap."

Titus looked around, marveling at the design. "The diagram does not do it justice."

"I consider myself to be a perfectionist," Dutch said arrogantly.

"How soon before we can begin?" Titus asked.

"Well, I would've liked to have a more stable power source," Dutch began, but when he saw the look on Titus's face, he changed his stance. "But I will make do with what we have to work with. The first *volunteer* is already in position." He motioned toward a woman whose arms were suspended over her head by a chain that hung from the ceiling. She was a pretty pecan-colored woman with dark eyes that stared murderously at Titus.

Tamalla P. Hardy was a clairvoyant, someone who communicated with the dead. As a kid, it had been the bane of her existence and cost her parents thousands of dollars in therapy, but when she got older, she learned to capitalize on her gift. She made a nice living trafficking between mortals and the dead. The events surrounding the reappearance of the Nimrod caused quite a stir in the Dead Lands, and Tamalla sought to use what she knew to turn a profit, but instead, it put her in the crosshairs of the dark order and at the mercy of Titus.

Titus removed the gag from her mouth. "Nice to see you again, Ms. Hardy."

"Titus, you double-crossing son of a bitch, what's this

about? You said if I helped you, I'd be rewarded, not taken prisoner!"

"And I will stay true to my word, Ms. Hardy," Titus assured her. With a wave of his hand, the chains that had been suspending her snapped and she fell limply into his waiting arms. He dragged her, kicking and screaming, to a chamber across the room and shoved her inside the glass prism. "For your greed and treachery, I shall grant you the greatest reward, by allowing you to serve as the spark that will set the world ablaze." Titus nodded at Dutch, who flipped a switch and activated the machine.

The crystal hummed to life, brighter as it charged. Tamalla looked up with tear-filled eyes, knowing she was living her final moments, but she never realized how painfully her end would come. A beam of white light poured from the crystal and burrowed into her forehead, drawing a horrid scream from her. The beam turned a sickly green before reversing itself and pulling Tamalla's soul from her body and into the Devil's Trap. As her soul was sucked out, the clock-like gears began to turn, which set in motion a series of smaller gears. Soon the quiet room was filled with the sounds of grinding metal mechanical noises and the crackling of the dark magic they had just tapped into.

Titus turned to Dutch. "The Trap is sprung. Now, do what you must to start the Rising." He turned next to Helena. "Make sure that souls are continuously fed into the Trap. Under no circumstances are you to stop, and if you run out of corpses, then you have my blessing to improvise as you see fit."

Helena looked around at the girls wearing the robes and licked her lips. "Now that sounds like it could be fun."

"This is no game, Helena. We must—" Titus's words

caught in his throat, and he dropped to one knee, clutching his chest.

Helena was immediately at his side and helped Titus to his feet. "What's wrong?"

Titus took a minute to catch his breath before responding. "We've got company."

• CHAPTER FIFTEEN •

Gabriel felt the cool rush of wind against his face. He felt free, almost euphoric. The wonderful sensation quickly gave way to pain as the ground slammed into his face. He moved to a sitting position, trying to orientate himself. He was groggy as if he had just awoken from a short nap. As near as he could tell, he was in a forest. Beyond the trees, he saw lights twinkling in a massive house. Slowly it came back to him, where he was and how he had gotten there. He had just passed through the rip! The shadows around him moved, and he was about to draw the Nimrod when he realized it was only the rest of his group.

"Damn, that hurt," DeMona said, lying on her back, looking up at the trees.

Rogue came out of the shrubs, picking leaves out of his dreadlocks. "Well, at least he didn't drop us over an ocean where we could've all drowned."

"At least it wouldn't have hurt as much," DeMona said.

"Is everyone accounted for?" Rogue asked, looking around for those he hadn't yet heard from. Slowly they all sounded off. Asha, Cristobel, Morgan, Gilgamesh—they were all accounted for. "Jonas, are you getting us on your GPS system?" He spoke into one of the modified Bluetooth devices that Jonas had provided them all with. They would not only allow the group to keep in contact, but would also tell Jonas their exact locations so he could help them navigate Raven Wood.

"Loud and clear, John." Jonas's voice came through each earpiece. "I've got you guys on the west end of the estate. Head east and it should run you directly into the main house. From the spectral energy I'm picking up from our eye in the sky, I'd say that's where the Rising is going to happen."

"Then that's the building we need to tear down." Morgan tightened his grip on his hammer.

"Watch your step, Red, we're also picking up heavy shithead activity." This was Jackson's voice now. Shitheads were the name he and Rogue had given to the Stalkers. He wasn't happy about being left behind, but he understood.

"Guess we may as well get moving." Gabriel started toward the house.

The group followed Gabriel through the woods surrounding Raven Wood, eyes and senses constantly alert for danger. When they reached the edge of the clearing between the shrubs and the house, they could get a better view of the layout. There were several guards milling about the front of the house as well as a regular patrol on the perimeter. Some looked human and some were clearly not, but they were all in the employ of the dark order. Less than five feet away from the stand of trees that hid Gabriel and the others was an unguarded door that led inside Raven Wood.

"When the next patrol passes, we should move for the door," Morgan suggested.

"Agreed. I'll go first," Cristobel offered. He took a step closer to the edge of the woods, and DeMona stopped him.

"Wait, something is wrong," Asha said.

Rogue scanned the woods with his shadow eyes. "I don't see anything."

"No, she's right." Mercy cocked her head to the side and listened. "Do you hear it?"

"I don't hear anything," Cristobel said.

"Exactly, it's too quiet. Even the woods have gone silent," Mercy explained.

The ground suddenly exploded into a spray of dirt as corpses rose up from the ground and attacked them. These Stalkers weren't like the ones they had faced in the city; they were stronger and faster.

"It's a trap!" Gabriel screamed, as one of the corpses grabbed him and pulled him into the ground.

"Gabriel!" Asha dove and grabbed him by the leg of his pants, and was dragged into the earth with him. The ground snapped closed behind them.

"No!" Mercy began to tear clumps of dirt from the ground with her claws, trying to get to them, but they were already gone.

Gabriel tumbled end over end through the loose dirt, dragged along by the Stalkers. His mouth and nose were filled with dirt as he was pulled deeper into the ground. He could feel the Stalkers clawing at his skin like they were trying to rip it from his bones. Suddenly the dirt beneath him opened up, and he was dropped onto a concrete floor. He managed to pull the Nimrod from his pants, but three Stalkers dove on him and pinned his arm and body to the ground, preventing him from striking with it. Gabriel grunted and bucked one of the Stalkers off him. He brought his fist around and slammed it into the skull of the one holding his other arm down, over and over until he finally released him. When his hand was free, he drove the two rusty points of the fork into the Stalker's eyes.

Gabriel scrambled out from under the pile of Stalkers and got to his feet, bloody fork in hand. It didn't take the Stalkers long to regroup and advance on him again. A few feet away from him, Asha fought against impossible numbers. For every Stalker struck down with her black dagger, it seemed like two more took their place. They soon overran her and wrestled Asha to the ground. Gabriel heard her scream from somewhere in the dogpile. He shook the Nimrod like a fading flashlight, pleading with it to work, but it remained silent.

Two of the Stalkers tackled Gabriel and pinned him to the wall. Two more joined in, and they tried to pull Gabriel down. He fought against them, but the Stalkers were too strong. He knew if he let them get him on the ground, it would be over for him and Asha. In the back of his mind, he heard what sounded like the Bishop snickering.

"I will not fail them again!" Gabriel bellowed. There was a flash of light, and the Nimrod appeared in all its glory. Gabriel pushed out with the force of his will, sending the Stalkers flying backward and crashing into the walls. He pointed the Nimrod at the Stalkers who were on Asha and called the lightning. The powerful bolts shot from the trident and turned the walking corpses into ash.

Asha slowly got off the ground and brushed soot from her clothes. "Nice move, Redfeather. I was starting to think you had forgotten how to use that thing."

"Me too," Gabriel admitted.

"Where the hell are we?" Asha looked around. They were in a cellar with thick stone walls and lined with unmarked boxes.

"I don't know, under the house somewhere. Let's see if Jonas can help us get out of here." Gabriel tapped his Bluetooth. "Jonas, are you there?" There was no answer, only static. "Nothing. Maybe you can reach him."

"Doubt it," Asha said while examining her earpiece, which had been fried by the lightning. "Looks like we're on our own."

Rogue and the others found themselves surrounded by the forces of hell. The Stalkers came at them fast and in numbers. He pulled out his enchanted revolver and fired into the wedge of Stalkers moving on them, scattering them from the impact of the bullet long enough to regroup. He was about to shout something to the others when Cristobel tackled him to the ground. Seconds later, a barrage of bullets tore through the ground where he had been standing.

"I owe you," Rogue told the dwarf.

"Nay, this almost makes us even," Cristobel told him.

There was another spray of bullets that tore up the dirt around where they lay. Rogue looked up, and in the darkness of a balcony, he saw a man holding a machine gun. "The balcony!" he shouted, pointing to the shooter.

"I'm on him." Mercy darted forward. She weaved between the bullets and launched into the air, claws extended. She landed on the rail of the balcony and found herself staring down the barrel of the machine gun.

The shooter squeezed the trigger and let the bullets fly. He peered through the gun smoke, expecting to see a corpse, but instead saw a pair of moonlit eyes glaring at him.

"When your boss hired you, he should've at least taught you how to kill what you're fighting, *human*." Mercy struck with her claws.

Below, DeMona was tearing into a Stalker, painting the side of the house with his blood when another one grabbed her from behind. He was incredibly strong, but she was stronger and showed him as much when she grabbed him by the wrists and broke both of his arms at the elbows. Even with its arms flapping uselessly at its sides, the Stalker continued to try and fight . . . until Gilgamesh took his head with Teko's blade.

"I'm glad you're better at killing people with that thing than you are opening rips," DeMona joked.

Gilgamesh's lips curved slightly at the corners. It was the closest she had seen him come to a smile since she had met him.

Something heavy landed on the ground between them. It was a human head. They both looked up at the same time to see Mercy perched on the balcony railing, giving them the thumbs-up before disappearing.

"I can only imagine what it must've been like growing up in your house," Gilgamesh said.

"No, you can't." DeMona wiped her claws on the clothes of the Stalker she had just slain.

"Get the lead out! We've got more company coming!" Rogue shouted to them. The commotion had alerted the armed guards who had been patrolling the house, and they were surging on them. Rogue broke for the door on the side of the house only to find his way blocked by more Stalkers crawling out of the ground. They were trapped.

"There are too many of them. We'll never reach the door," Cristobel said, clutching his axe.

"Then I will provide us with another," Morgan said, smashing his hammer into the side of the house, caving in the wall. "This way," he urged them.

They all spilled through the hole in the wall to the inside of Raven Wood with their enemies hot on their heels. When they were all safely through, Rogue erected a wall of shadows to cover their escape.

"I don't know how long that'll hold them, so I suggest we keep moving," Rogue said.

A voice spoke up. "I think it's best if you all stay where you are." They turned to see the war demon Riel standing in the center of the room, holding his cursed blade, Poison. With him were a dozen mortals, all armed with various automatic weapons.

DeMona sighed. "Not you again."

"What's the matter? Aren't you happy to see me?" Riel asked.

"I'm as happy to see you as a hooker leaving the free clinic with bad news," DeMona snapped.

"Friend of yours?" Gilgamesh asked DeMona.

"Hardly. More like a herpes outbreak because he just keeps popping up."

"I would encourage you to lower your weapons, or I'll have my men cut you down," Riel warned.

"I'm gonna eat those bullets right before I make you eat that gun," DeMona snarled.

"You may be bulletproof, Valkrin, but can the same be said of your friends?" Riel asked, and ordered his men to train the guns on the others. "Now, you are free to gamble, but keep in mind that the stakes are for the lives of your friends."

"Drop 'em," Rogue ordered the others.

Gilgamesh refused. "The hell I will. If I'm gonna die, I'm gonna go out in a blaze of glory."

"Yeah and take everybody else with you. Know when to pick your battles, Mesh." Rogue winked. Reluctantly, Gilgamesh and the others lowered their weapons.

Riel laughed. "You humans aren't as dumb as you look." He stood watch while the armed men secured Rogue and the others. "Now that we've gotten the pleasantries out of the way, I'd like to welcome you all to Raven Wood, your final resting place."

"Rogue, I sure hope you've got a plan," Morgan whispered, as they were marched through the hall.

"Indeed, I do," Rogue said.

"Well, don't keep an asshole in suspense. What is it?" DeMona asked.

"Keep these fucks busy long enough for Gabriel and Asha to destroy the Devil's Trap and save us," Rogue said.

"That's your plan?" Gilgamesh looked at him as if he had completely lost his mind. "That human is an idiot and has almost gotten us killed several times in the few hours I've known him, and you're depending on him to save the day?"

"Gabriel might not be a soldier, or even the most skilled of us, but he's resilient. I know there's a hero hiding in that boney frame somewhere. He'll come through." Rogue sounded surer than he actually was.

"You'd better hope so, because if he doesn't, I'm gonna kill you long before Titus has a chance to feed you to the Devil's Trap."

Mercy watched the battle below from her perch on the balcony railing. She was about to rejoin the fight when she felt a presence behind her. When she turned, she was face to face with someone whom she had until recently called sister and friend. The second Valkrin, Alicia, who had come to New York with her to serve as Titus's bodyguards.

"Hello, traitor," Alicia greeted her before plunging her sword into Mercy's gut.

Mercy's eyes went wide with shock. Her blood began to burn like someone had injected her with acid. She opened her mouth to speak, but couldn't get enough air into her lungs to get the words out.

"Dragon's blood," Alicia explained, twisting the sword in Mercy's gut. "Lethal to most, but it only paralyzes our kind, and the effects are only temporary." She looked Mercy in the eyes. "I can tell by your facial expression that if you could, you would rip my heart out and feast on it, and there is no doubt in my mind that you could if it had been a fair fight. That's why I chose the sneaky route. Yes, I know it violates our oldest rules of combat, but the old ways are dead and a new era is upon us. No longer will my sisters and I be the foot soldiers of the dark order, but the generals of all armies, and Titus will make it so."

"Kill . . . you . . ." Mercy managed to force out before the poison atrophied her jaw muscles.

"Of this, I'm sure, but you'll never have the chance. I've got big plans for you, Mercy, very big plans. Your powerful spirit should be just what my lord Titus needs," Alicia taunted. Six robed women came onto the balcony and flanked Alicia. "Take her below and feed her to the Trap with the others."

• CHAPTER SIXTEEN •

"What the hell is going on down there?" Jackson asked frantically, listening to the audio feed through the speakers in the room.

"I'm trying to figure it out." Jonas's fingers moved swiftly across the keyboard. "Our people are in the thick of it, and I've lost contact with Gabriel and Asha altogether." He was getting nervous but tried his best to stay composed for the sake of Lydia and Finnious, who looked terrified.

"Somebody better tell me something, or I'm gonna go out there and find out myself," Jackson threatened. He'd felt in his gut that it was a bad idea for them to attack Raven Wood in full force, but he was outvoted.

"Jackson, you're still not one hundred percent, and even if you were, there's no way you'd be able to get to Raven Wood in time to be of much help," Jonas told him. "We've got to be calm and hope that our people can get the situation back under control. If not, we must succeed where they've failed."

"This is bad, all bad," Finnious said.

"It's going to be okay." Lydia tried to put her arm around him, but it passed through. When Finnious was nervous, his body phased in and out.

Finnious was listening to Lydia's reassuring words when he felt something crawl across his skin. It was like a marching of ants. The Spark in his gut began to burn, alerting him of danger. "Someone is here," he said, looking around nervously.

Lydia was immediately on her feet, spear in hand, listening for anything out of place in the room.

Jonas took a minute to examine all of the video monitors and his early warning systems. All seemed quiet. "Finnious, I think it's just your nerves. I don't see anything."

"It's not my nerves." Finnious began moving back toward a corner in the room. "They're all around us, we're gonna die!" He whipped his head back and forth, looking around nervously, searching for something.

"Calm down, Finnious. Nobody is here but us," Jonas assured him.

"No, no, no. They're all around us. All is lost, don't you feel them?" Finnious pressed.

"Who, kid?" Jackson asked, unsheathing his arm blades. He didn't see anything either, but Finnious's outburst had him on edge.

"Them!" Finnious pointed to a dark corner on the far side of the room.

All eyes turned to where he was pointing. At first there was nothing, and then the space he was pointing at began to waver, like looking through an open flame. Then they appeared, one by one, ghostly shades dressed in ancient Egyptian garbs and carrying blades. Leading them was a man who sported a bald head with a long braid that hung down his back. His white eyes scanned the room until they landed on Finnious and the thing that pulsed within him.

"The Sheut!" Jonas gasped.

The Sheut were the notorious crew of Egyptian pirates who had originally stolen the Nimrod from King Neptune for the death god Thanos. Their mission was thwarted when they were captured by the church's Templar Knights and burned alive along with their ship, the *Jihad*, but this was not to be the end of the pirates. Instead of letting their souls pass into the afterlife, Thanos punished them for their failure by cursing them to serve as the ferrymen to the dead, transporting souls between the here and there. For centuries, Ezrah had been searching for a way to break the curse, and he found it when Angelo passed the Spark to Finnious.

Ezrah pointed his curved saber at Finnious. "Bring me the Spark," he ordered.

The wraiths surged forward, eager to do their master's bidding.

"Don't touch him." Lydia threw herself in front of Finnious, seeking to cut him off from the attacking wraiths. She struck with the Spear of Truth, but it passed through the wraiths harmlessly. Before she could recover, the wraith closest to her stuck its hand in her chest. Lydia's body was assaulted with a bone-chilling cold, and she dropped like a stone, trembling.

The wraith stepped over Lydia and continued toward Finnious. "Give it," he demanded.

"Sure thing," Jonas called from behind him. He was holding

a strange-looking gun. It looked like a cheese grater attached to the end of an assault rifle.

The wraith smirked. "Bullets are useless against ghosts."

"Then it's a good thing I loaded this with something else." Jonas pulled the trigger. The gun fired off a beam of green light, and when it made contact with the wraith, its form wavered then turned in on itself and vanished. The gun was one of Jonas's latest inventions, created specifically to disperse spectral energy. He had never tested it until then and had no idea if it would actually work, but he was thankful it did. Jonas turned to the other wraiths, leveling the gun. "Okay, who's next?"

Several of the wraiths came at Jonas. The first two fell victim to the gun, but when he tried to fire on the others, the weapon fizzled and short-circuited. The remaining wraiths closed in on Jonas, but Jackson stepped between them.

"Now, do you really think I'm going to let you kill my buddy?" Jackson asked. Both his arm blades were fully extended. The wraiths formed a tight circle around him and Jonas. "These odds are more to my liking." He looked around at them.

"You are a fool, human. Your steel blades will do you no good against the Sheut," one of the wraiths told him. "Take him."

The wraiths closed in to finish Jackson. Jackson spun, blades swinging, and laid into the wraiths, reducing them to clouds of smoke as he struck. The wraith who had been taunting him looked on in disbelief.

"Impossible. Steel cannot destroy a ghost," the wraith insisted.

"Who said my blades were made of steel?" Jackson asked before destroying the wraith. "Cold iron, baby, the original

Ghostbuster," he said smugly. "Now I'm gonna—" Jackson's words were cut off and his face twisted into a mask of pain. He dropped to his knees, face frozen in shock. Behind him, Ezrah stood with his hand palming the back of Jackson's head.

"I'm tired of these games. I will have the Spark, and all of you will ride the *Jihad*," Ezrah said triumphantly.

"Leave him alone." Finnious moved to face Ezrah. His hands were glowing with power.

Ezrah released Jackson and turned to Finnious. "Little brother, it had been my hope to spare you after I took what I needed, but you are leaving me little choice. If you wish to die with these mortals, then so be it, but first you will kneel before the future king of the Dead Lands." He raised his hand and tried to exercise his will over Finnious as he had done with other wraiths, but nothing happened. "I don't understand. No wraith is beyond my control."

"I am only half wraith," Finnious corrected him and laid his hands on Ezrah's chest. Light poured from Finnious's hands and filled Ezrah's body. When the ferryman opened his mouth to scream, light poured from it like vomit, running down his body.

Computers and monitors alike began to blink on and off. Wires sparked and caught fire so fast that Jonas barely had time to extinguish them. It was as if Finnious were causing some type of short circuit throughout the whole system.

"Finnious, what are you doing?" Jonas shouted.

"I don't know. I can't make it stop," Finnious said nervously.

There was a loud popping sound followed by an explosion of light that sent Finnious and Ezrah flying in opposite directions. Finnious slammed into the wall with so much force that he thought he'd cracked his skull. The last thing he remembered was seeing Ezrah's body lying on the ground, smoldering, before everything went black.

When Finnious awoke, the first face he saw was Jackson's. Ever since he'd felt the dark presence, he'd developed a measure of dislike for Jackson, but at that moment he had never been happier to see him. The fact that he was able to see anything meant that he was still alive. Finnious tried to sit up, but Jackson bid him to stay down.

"Easy, kid. You've been through a lot. Don't wanna rush it," Jackson told him.

Finnious nodded. "Where's Lydia?"

"I'm here," she said from the chair next to his bedside. She had a thick blanket draped over her shoulders and a cup of hot chocolate in her hands.

"What happened?" Finnious asked.

"We were hoping you could tell us. What do you remember about what happened?" Jonas asked.

"I don't know. I remember being scared when the fighting started, and I was trying to find someplace to hide. When I saw Ezrah hurt Lydia then trying to hurt you and Jackson, I knew I couldn't let it happen."

Jonas nodded in understanding, but couldn't hide the worry on his face. "And Ezrah? What did you do to him?"

"I don't know what I did to Ezrah. Jonas, what's going on?" Finnious was confused.

Jonas looked at Jackson, who simply shrugged. "I think I can show you better than I can tell you." He extended his hand. Finnious reluctantly took it.

Jonas led Finnious out of the room and across the hall to another room, which had a digital lock on the door. After

Jonas punched in a combination, the door clicked open and they stepped inside. Finnious felt a chill deep in his bones as if they had just stepped into a meat locker. At the back of the room, he could see a glowing rectangle that looked like a big fish tank with someone standing in the center.

"Who is that?" Finnious asked.

"See for yourself." Jonas flipped the light switch and illuminated the room. In the light, Finnious could see who it was standing in the rectangle. It was Ezrah, but something about him was off. When Finnious looked at him with his senses and not his eyes, he realized what was off about him. He was no longer a ghost, he was human.

When Ezrah noticed Finnious, he flew into a rage, hurling himself at the glass that held him and banging against it. "What have you done to me? Tell me, you sneaky little half-breed. How did you do it? How did you steal my power?" There were tears running down his face.

"Oh my God, how?" Finnious covered his mouth. "Did I do this?"

"Apparently so. I have never seen anything like this and can't find anything similar in all of my databases," Jonas admitted. "I was hoping you could shed some light on it."

"I swear, I don't know. You have to believe me," Finnious said.

"I do believe you, Fin. I'm just stumped, and the fact that you don't know how you did it raises even more questions. If you don't mind, I'd like to run some tests on you."

"You'll not be turning Finnious into one of your lab rats," Lydia told Jonas, hugging Finnious to her defensively.

Jonas raised his hands showing that he meant no harm. "I would never try to use Finnious as a lab rat, but none of us are clear as to the extent or limits of his abilities. I'm just curious to know what affect the Spark had on his already *unique* condition."

"We can play mad scientist later. Have you all forgotten that our people are currently at Raven Wood getting their asses kicked?" Jackson reminded them.

"You're right. Let's get back to the control room." Jonas led them out.

"Don't walk away from me! I need answers!" Ezrah shouted, still banging on the glass. "Why did you do this to me? Why? I demand to know!"

As they were leaving the room, Finnious stopped short and looked back at the rectangle. Ezrah had tired himself out and was on the floor weeping. Though Ezrah had tried to destroy him, his heart went out to the ferryman. He knew what it was like not to understand what you were and not be able to look to anyone for answers. "I am truly sorry," Finnious whispered before moving to catch up with the others.

· CHAPTER SEVENTEEN ·

Gabriel and Asha crept through the halls of Raven Wood. Asha's plan sounded like a good one, but once he agreed to go along with it, he wasn't so sure.

"Asha, I don't know about this," Gabriel whispered to her.

"Be quiet and let me concentrate. It's taking a lot out of me to hold this spell together," Asha told him. She had cast a spell that would render them almost invisible to humans unless someone was looking directly at them. To her credit, it was working so far, but Gabriel still felt like a walking target.

"Okay, but we still don't know where we're going," Gabriel pointed out.

"Hey, do I have to do everything around here? Why don't you ask your little friend where we should be going?" she was referring to the Bishop.

"How about it? Do you know where we're going?" Gabriel asked sarcastically.

Probably to your deaths if you don't free me and I do what must be done, the Bishop told him.

"Not gonna happen," Gabriel said.

Have it your way, but when Titus relieves you of your head, you'll wish you had listened, the Bishop warned.

Two men armed with rifles were coming down the hall from the opposite direction. Trailing behind them were three shambling corpses, being pulled along by the chains wrapped around their necks. Gabriel and Asha immediately stopped moving and pressed themselves against the wall. One of the Stalkers stopped short and turned its dead eyes to Gabriel and Asha. They were exposed. Gabriel was about to summon the Nimrod from his arm, but Asha stayed his hand.

"Get the lead out, you fucking zombie!" One of the men crashed the butt of his rifle into the side of the Stalker's head. He was standing less than a foot from Gabriel and Asha but didn't seem to notice them.

"Quit abusing the merchandise," the second man said.

"These things don't feel shit." He shot the Stalker in the arm, splattering blood on Gabriel and Asha. "See? Nothing."

"Whatever, just quit playing and come on. We've got to get these three downstairs. I don't want Titus or any of his henchmen on my ass because you're dawdling."

"Those fucking guys give me the creeps. I especially hate that prissy fucker Flagg," the first man admitted.

"For as much money as they're paying us, you can hate them, as long as we get the job done," the second man told him. "Now, come on, they're waiting for these three to feed them to the Devil's Trap with the others."

"A nasty piece of work, that Devil's Trap," the first man said.

"Indeed it is. Just be glad they're feeding these soulless fucks to it instead of us," the second man said.

"Hopefully, it'll be over soon. I hear they've just brought in some fresh meat."

"Yeah, a bunch of dumb fucks who thought they'd be able to storm Raven Wood. Flagg says that feeding them to the Devil's Trap should provide them with enough juice to get this show on the road," the second man explained.

"I almost feel sorry for them, but hey, better them than us. I know I've got first dibs on their weapons. I wanna see what kinda damage I can do with those two funky revolvers the Black guy was carrying."

The second man walked up on the first. "Let me give you some advice: If you plan to live long enough to spend the money Titus is giving us, then I suggest you keep your hands and eyes to yourself."

"Stop being such a stick-in-the-mud. Who's gonna miss two little pistols?" the first man argued.

"You heard what I said, and if you do anything to put us on Titus's bad side, I'll kill you myself. Now, less talking and more walking." The men exchanged a few more words before continuing down the hall.

"Did you hear that?" Asha asked.

"Yes. They've got our people," Gabriel said.

"What now?"

"We keep fighting," Gabriel said as if it shouldn't have been a question. "We're gonna follow the Stalkers to the Devil's Trap and put an end to this once and for all." Gabriel headed down the hall after the Stalkers.

"Or die trying," Asha added before joining him.

One by one, Riel marched the Stalkers into the chamber and watched as the Devil's Trap drained them of their souls. After each soul was sucked out, the robed women would clear the chamber of the empty shell and make it ready for the next one. Dutch stood on a podium, chanting the words of power, which would raise the twelve from the dead, while Flagg attended the host bodies. Already the twelve vessels in the sarcophagi began to show signs of life, and it wouldn't be long before they walked again and Titus would have his generals. The Rising was complete, and victory was almost at hand.

Titus stood in the center of the Devil's Trap, smiling like the cat who had just swallowed the canary. Kneeling before him, bound and held in place by chains that were bolted to the floor, were the mighty champions: the mage, the elemental, the dark elf, the dwarf, and the two Valkrin. Gabriel and the blood witch weren't among them, but it didn't matter. Once he had drained the others and completed the Rising, there would be nothing left to stop him, not even the Nimrod.

"How the mighty have fallen," Titus said, looking over their angry faces.

"Why don't you kill us already and spare us from having to hear your annoying ass voice any longer?" DeMona said defiantly.

Titus slapped her viciously across the face. "Hold your tongue, demon."

Mercy tried to jump to her feet, but the chains holding her to the ground were too strong for even her to break. "Touch my child again and I'll rip your heart out."

Alicia kicked her in the back and sent her spilling to the ground. "You'll do nothing except die to further my master's gains."

Mercy slowly got herself to a sitting position. She cast her eyes on Alicia. "I'm gonna rip his heart out, but you, sister, I will kill very slowly."

"You'll pass through to the Dead Lands long before me, Mercy," Alicia assured her. She turned to Titus. "If it pleases my lord, we will feed her to the Trap next."

Titus nodded. Alicia cut Mercy again with the dragon blood–soaked blade, so that she wouldn't give them any trouble while the robed women released her chains from the floor. Her eyes held hatred and contempt, but there was nothing she could do to act on it. Carefully, they carried the Valkrin to the chamber and placed her inside.

"Mother!" DeMona fought against the chains. The stones that held the chain rocked back and forth in the ground as she tugged at them. Two of the humans in Titus's employ had to restrain her to ensure she didn't break free.

Mercy made eye contact with her daughter from inside the chamber. Even on the cusp of her own destruction, her eyes were still proud and fierce. Something unspoken passed between mother and daughter before Mercy turned her eyes toward the crystal, prepared to face her end with dignity.

"Behold the power of the Devil's Trap," Titus said smugly, and gave Flagg the signal to activate the crystal. As it had with Tamalla, the beam poured forth and burrowed into Mercy. Unlike the clairvoyant's, her soul would not be parted with her body so easily. It took almost a full five minutes before she stopped moving.

Seeing her mother's lifeless body being dragged from the chamber drained all the fight from DeMona, and she collapsed, resting her forehead on the ground and weeping. "Mother."

Alicia laughed. "Don't worry, little one, you'll join your mother soon enough."

Without warning, DeMona's head shot up. One of the human guards who had been restraining her was caught completely by surprise when she bit into his arm and ripped loose a chunk from his bicep. With a grunt, she tore one of her arms free and grabbed for Alicia, who jumped back. The room was thrown into chaos, but Titus remained calm, as he raised his hand and released his power. DeMona flew backward, slamming into the wall. Titus walked up to her and stood over the dazed demon.

"Foolish, foolish child. Don't you know that you have no hope of defeating me?" Titus asked.

DeMona rolled over onto her stomach and spat the flesh she'd ripped from the man at Titus's feet. "For as long as there is good in the world, there will always be hope."

Titus kicked DeMona in the face and knocked her out. "Load her in next."

Rogue had seen enough. "Titus, this is madness. Do you know what will happen if you raise the twelve and the Devil's Trap fails to bind them to your will?"

Titus shrugged. "They'll likely go mad and lay waste to this world and everyone in it. Either way, the age of man ends tonight."

Just then, the two guards who had been escorting the last of the Stalkers entered the room. "Line them up against the wall with the rest," Riel ordered. One by one, the humans marched the Stalkers to the other side of the room. When the last one passed, something caught Riel's eyes. "Wait, what the—" That was as far as he got before Gabriel buried the Nimrod in his chest.

They had agreed to wait until the time was right to strike so as to keep their only advantage, which was the element of surprise, but when Gabriel saw Titus and thought of his grandfather, something inside him snapped. He wasn't sure if it was the manipulation of the Bishop or his own impulsiveness, but he knew that Titus had to die.

Riel was a powerful demon, but he was caught off guard and never stood a chance. The Nimrod sunk into his chest with a sickening noise, and Gabriel lifted him off his feet. "So we meet again, demon, but I fear this will be for the final time." He called the lightning. Riel's body shook violently at the end of the Nimrod. The demon was forced from its host, which was now reduced to little more than a charred husk. Without Riel to animate them, the Stalkers dropped and the spirits within them returned to the grave where they belonged. Gabriel tossed the corpse to the side then set his sights on Titus.

"I thought you'd be somewhere with your head buried in the sand, waiting for the end to come." Titus drew his blade.

"No more running. We finish this. I will not let you have this world, Titus," Gabriel said.

"*Let me?* Silly boy, this world is already mine." Titus swung his blade.

He and Gabriel exchanged strikes, sending sparks of magic flying. The mortals who had been hired to do Titus's bidding decided that it was a good time to turn in their resignations and fled, including the mage Flagg, who had slipped out as soon as the fighting started. For as loyal as he was to Titus, he was more loyal to himself.

Gabriel was so focused on Titus that he didn't notice the vampire Helena creep up on him. She locked her arm around Gabriel's neck, cutting off his air. "You will not stop us, mortal," she breathed into his face. Helena pulled his head back and exposed his neck. "I will drink deeply—" Her words cut off. Helena yelled before her body crumbled to ash. When

Gabriel finally caught his breath, he looked up and saw Asha standing over him, holding her black dagger.

"Thanks, Asha," he rasped.

"Thank me by kicking Titus's ass," she told him.

Gabriel rolled to his feet and reengaged Titus. Titus tore into Gabriel fiercely, but this time Gabriel wasn't afraid and he stood his ground, giving just as good as he got.

"Someone has found his courage, I see." Titus struck twice with his sword, with Gabriel barely blocking the blows. "It won't change the fact that you're going to die."

"As long as I can take you with me, I'm cool with that." Gabriel tried to spear Titus, but he moved at the last minute and brought his sword down, opening up a nasty cut on Gabriel's arm. Asha moved to help Gabriel, but he waved her away. "Stop the Rising," he told her while keeping his focus on Titus.

Asha and Dutch spotted each other at the same time. Dutch stepped down off the podium and rolled up the sleeves of the black robe he was wearing. "Asha, thank the Goddess. I thought you had—"

She cut him off. "Save it. Lisa and Lane told me everything before I killed them."

Dutch sighed. "Asha, I did what I did for the betterment of the coven. You understand, don't you?"

"You care nothing about the coven, Dutch. Only your own greedy needs. I looked up to you and remained loyal even when my heart told me I shouldn't have, and you repaid me by sending my best friends to kill me. All I want to know is, why?"

"For power, why else?" Dutch said honestly. "You were too close to the truth, and I had to quiet you before my secret got out. You may not like what I did, but one as ambitious as you should understand."

"I understand nothing except you're a piece of shit and everything you've ever told me is a lie," she said emotionally.

"Not everything, Asha. You are truly one of my most gifted people, and the fact that despite my best efforts you have survived means that you are worthy to stand at my side as we usher in a new age of magic." He extended his hand. Behind his back, he held a knife.

Asha moved forward, standing before him and weighing his words. Even though Dutch had betrayed her, there was a part of her that loved him, and she wanted to believe there was some truth in his words, but she knew better. Asha lashed out and cut his hand with the black dagger. "Fool me once, shame on you. Fool me twice, and you burn!" She forced the power into her words.

Dutch felt the first licks of pain in his hand as Asha's magic took effect. "You ungrateful mongrel! I took you in; made sure you had an education—"

"And you also ripped my heart out and stomped on it when you betrayed me and the Black Court. But as they say, turnabout is fair play. Now stop crying and burn!" She forced more power into the spell. She had brought the mighty Black King to his knees and was about to finish him when she felt the cold touch of steel against her neck. "Fuck," was all Asha could say.

Gabriel's muscles throbbed, and he wanted to quit, but he knew that if he did, all would be lost and this alone kept him fighting. Titus was more skilled than he in combat, but Gabriel was going off raw emotion.

Titus swung in a high arch, expecting Gabriel to duck the blow, but instead, he met it head on with the trident. Magic flared as the two weapons connected. Gabriel and Titus were nose to nose, each trying to gain ground. In the light of the magic, Titus could see the storm clouds rolling in his young opponent's eyes. For the first time, Titus wasn't certain about his victory.

Yes, kill him! Slay the betrayer! the Bishop ordered.

Using his foot, Titus pushed off Gabriel's chest and broke the lock. He swung wildly with his blade, with Gabriel deflecting the strikes and countering with an uppercut to the gut that lifted Titus slightly off his feet. Titus tried to raise his sword, but Gabriel brought the shaft of the Nimrod down across his wrist, knocking his sword from his hand.

"Now, we finish this," Gabriel said in a voice that was not totally his own. Pointing the Nimrod at Titus, he let loose the lightning. Currents of electricity raced through every muscle in Titus's body, bringing on a seizure. Titus flicked around on the ground, foaming from the mouth and whimpering. Gabriel's heart was touched with remorse, but it quickly faded when the sharp words of the Bishop cut through his skull like a heated knife.

If he lives, neither you nor those you love will ever know peace. It ends with his life, the Bishop nudged.

Gabriel raised the trident high above his head. "Then let what was begun be finished." Before the strike fell, Gabriel heard a voice boom.

"Lay one more hand on him, and your friend dies!" Alicia said. She was holding Asha with the blade to her throat, prepared to split her open.

"Don't you do it, Gabriel. You kill that son of a bitch!" Asha shouted.

Gabriel paused. He had lost so many already and didn't have the heart to watch someone else he cared about die. "Okay, just let her go." Gabriel backed away from Titus.

It's a trick; she'll kill the girl anyway. What is one life measured against the billions you'll save? the Bishop asked.

"I wouldn't expect someone like you to understand," Gabriel told the Bishop while laying the Nimrod on the ground.

Someone like me? You fool yourself, boy. We are more alike than you give credit for. You lack the desire, but not the will to do what must be done. Concede and continue to fight me, and those who fought and died for you will have done so in vain. Or release the storm and cleanse this world of Titus's evil once and for all. Make your choice, the Bishop said and went silent again.

"Quit mumbling to yourself and get into the chamber," Alicia ordered him.

Rogue and the others watched in despair as Gabriel walked into the chamber, and Alicia closed it behind him. It was all over, and they knew it.

"Activate the crystal," Titus told Dutch, who eagerly obliged.

Gabriel watched as the crystal powered up. He looked to his friends, who wore various expressions of defeat and disappointment. He thought of his grandfather, who had given his life so that he could continue the fight, only to have him willingly give himself to Titus's whims. That was becoming the story of his life, giving into the wants of those who weren't important and failing those who were. This was not the mark he wanted to leave on the world. If this was the last hand of the game, then Gabriel intended to bet it all.

"I'm sorry, Granddad. This was the only way," he whispered, slowly dropping his mental defenses and opening his soul to the trident and the spirit trapped within it. "Thy will be done!" he shouted, and the chamber was flooded with light.

Titus found himself temporarily blinded when light came pouring out of the chamber. When his vision cleared, there was no sign of the Nimrod. When he looked to see where it had gotten to, he spotted it inside the chamber with Gabriel, or what was once Gabriel.

"Dutch, the crystal, hurry!" Titus shouted.

Dutch threw the switch and activated the Devil's Trap. The beam shot down into the chamber, striking the Nimrod instead of Gabriel. When the two forces combined, it caused a great explosion that rocked Raven Wood to its foundation. The Devil's Trap was destroyed and so was the magic that surrounded Raven Wood. The old house began to cave in, and fires began to break out. With the destruction of the Devil's Trap, the hold Titus had over the souls of the First Guard was also broken.

"No, no, no!" Titus screamed.

"Yes." Gabriel stepped from the chamber, smiling. He looked down at his arms as if he were feeling them for the first time. "After centuries of being trapped in corporal prison, I am free. I am flesh once more!" he said in a voice that wasn't his own.

"The Bishop!" Titus gasped.

"Yes, old friend. I walk once more, and that means you die, for good this time." He marched toward Titus.

Titus attacked with his sword, but unlike Gabriel, the Bishop was a master at combat. He swatted Titus's blows away playfully. "After four centuries, is that all that you have learned, other than suckling at your master's cock?"

Titus roared and swung his blade overhand with everything he had. When his jeweled sword made contact with the Nimrod, it shattered, leaving him defenseless. The Bishop lifted Titus from the ground by his throat, lightning crackling around his hand. "Let that which was once parted be whole again." He touched the Nimrod to Titus's chest. Titus's flesh split open like a rotten tomato, and the piece of the trident that had been lodged there all these years seeped out and took its rightful place at the head of the Nimrod.

Titus hung in the Bishop's hand weakly. His skin began to wrinkle and his hair thinned. The shard in his chest had been the only thing sustaining him throughout the centuries, and now that it was no longer a part of him, he began to age rapidly.

"Now, let us finish what we started all those centuries ago." The Bishop drove the Nimrod into Titus's stomach and pinned him to the wall.

Titus gasped, blood poured from his mouth and nose, and the power of the Nimrod surged through his decaying body. "You think you've succeeded in stopping me?" Titus laughed. "Fool, the Rising is complete and the First Guard will still rise."

"Yes, they will, but it will not be the dark order that they serve. Farewell, my brother, and may heaven snatch your soul from the pits of hell so that you may finally know peace." He forced the Nimrod up through Titus's gut until its points pierced his heart and ended the feud that had gone on between them for four hundred years.

Alicia watched in horror as Titus's dead husk fell to the ground. She looked to Dutch, but the warlock was long gone.

This was her cue to leave. She tossed Asha to the ground and made her way to the door, only to find her path blocked by DeMona.

"Nah, you ain't getting off that easily." DeMona drove her talons into Alicia's chest and took a firm hold of her heart. "This is for my mother, you bitch," she said before ripping the still beating muscle from her chest. Alicia fell to the ground, lifeless eyes staring off into space. To add insult to injury, DeMona brought her foot down and crushed Alicia's skull.

DeMona walked almost in a daze across the room to where her mother's body lay on the floor. Even in death, she was still the most beautiful woman she had ever seen. She dropped to her knees and held the heart over Mercy's lips. "I wasn't always the best daughter and didn't offer you much in life, which is probably why you left us, but in death, I give you the blood of your enemies." She burst the heart, letting the blood flow over Mercy's still lips. "If you see Daddy, tell him that I miss him and not to worry. I'll be okay." She placed a kiss on her mother's forehead. "I love you, Mommy."

Asha knelt beside Rogue and began working on the lock of his chain. "Did you miss me, handsome?" she asked him playfully.

"You sure took your time about it. Now hurry up and spring me so we can get out of here. This place is about to come down around our ears, and I don't wanna be around when it does."

"I'm trying, damn it. Give a girl a chance," Asha said, working feverishly. Something whistled past her head and the chain snapped. Asha looked up and saw DeMona standing over. "Jesus, why don't you make some noise when you walk?" Asha tried to make a joke, but DeMona ignored her and moved to free the others. "What's her problem?" Asha asked Rogue.

"She just lost her mom. Give her a break," Rogue said.

"I'm sorry," Asha said sincerely. She too knew the scars losing a parent could leave, and it wasn't a wound that healed quickly.

"I know you didn't mean anything by it, Asha. Let's just get our people and go." Rogue stood. He approached Gabriel, who was still standing over Titus's corpse, staring at it. "Good job, kid." He laid his hand on Gabriel's shoulder, but snatched it back when a shock ran up his arm. "Jesus, are you okay?" Rogue blew on his fingers to cool them from the burning.

Gabriel turned to face Rogue and storm clouds danced in his eyes. "Never felt better."

"Gabriel?" Rogue asked, sensing something was off with him.

"Guess again." Gabriel turned to the sarcophagi containing the host vessels of the First Guard and began cracking them open. One by one, the vessels began waking from their slumber.

Morgan and the others had retrieved their weapons and came to join Rogue, all wondering what was going on. "What in God's name are you doing?" Morgan asked.

"God? That's laughable," Gabriel said. "For too long God has been silent and let the people of the world destroy the paradise He created. I have come to wash away the sins of man. Those who do not stand with us will drown in the blood of the evildoer. Behold—" Gabriel started, but his words froze. It was if something had paralyzed him.

"I don't think that will happen, at least not for a very long time," a new voice spoke up. Everyone watched in amazement as an elderly man with white hair appeared seemingly out of nowhere.

"Aren't you the old dude from the alley?" DeMona asked, remembering the stranger who had approached right before she had met Gabriel. She thought the homeless old kook was trying to mug her.

"I have been many things over the millennia. These days, I am just a poor soul trying to right a grievous wrong," the white-haired old man said, strolling around the room. "Back to rest, brothers, and forgive me for allowing your slumber to be disturbed," he whispered as he touched each of the sarcophagi. One by one, the vessels went still again. With a wave of his hands, the old man raised the trapped souls from their bodies. They looked like flickering Christmas lights. He muttered something in a language nearly as old as time itself and just like that the lights vanished. They restless spirits were finally able to cross over into the deadlands where they belonged.

The old man turned to Gabriel and shook his head sadly. "My greatest accomplishment and my greatest failure." He plucked the Nimrod from Gabriel's hands and studied it. It pulsed with soft white light. After gorging on carnage for the last few days, the weapon finally seemed sated. "Your work is done, sleep now and I'll ensure you're never disturbed again," he told the trident. The old man turned back to Gabriel. "And you, Bishop, where do I begin? You were trusted to protect humanity, and instead, you almost destroyed it. I have only myself to blame for being naïve enough to believe that noble hearts were immune to corruption. No matter, your purpose here is done." He pursed his lips and blew, dispersing Gabriel's body like a sand castle caught in a strong wind.

"What the hell did you do?" Rogue asked in a heated tone, eyes on the few flakes of debris left that had once been Gabriel Redfeather.

"What I should have four centuries ago." The old man's voice was heavy with regret. "How could I have been so wrong?" he asked himself while studying what was left of the Devil's Trap.

"Mister, I don't know who you are, but you just turned a friend of mine into dust. Me and you are about to dance." Rogue raised his hands to call the shadows, but nothing happened.

"You should really be more mindful of how much access you give him," the old man said over his shoulder, continuing to examine the wreckage of the Devil's Trap. "Demons are tricky, and especially good at letting mortals foolish enough to traffic with them believe they're in control until it's too late. The demon you share skin with is one of the cagier ones. And you need not fear for Gabriel. His fate was chosen the moment he allowed the Nimrod to taste his essence. It would've never truly allowed them to be parted without destroying him, and even I wouldn't have been able to stop that."

"So, if you didn't destroy him with his body, where is his soul?" Morgan asked.

The old man looked at him as if the question was an insane one. "Resting in the bosom of his lover, where else?" He raised the Nimrod. "The trident is greedy and demanded a companion in exchange for going back to sleep. We saw what happened when it was paired with the Bishop, so another had to be chosen. Gabriel was the lesser of two evils, so to speak."

"Who the hell are you?" Asha asked the question that was on everyone's lips.

"I think I know." Cristobel had finally figured out what he

should've known all along. He stepped forward. He got down on one knee and bowed. "My people still talk about you and what you did for us to this day."

"Please get up, you're making me uncomfortable." The old man helped Cristobel to his feet. "Praises such as those are reserved for gods, and I am hardly a god, simply someone who wanted to give the world a gift."

"Okay, am I the only one who is lost?" Rogue asked.

Cristobel turned to Rogue. "We call him the Magician, because we know no other name for him. He was the one who, with my ancestors, helped to create the Trident of Heaven and give it life."

The Magician shrugged. "It's the short version, but accurate. Many years ago, I saw the fighting that had plagued the world and wanted to do something about it, so I helped to create a weapon that would end it, the Nimrod." He hoisted the trident. "I thought if placed in the right hands, it could bring an end to the wars that were ravaging the lands, but I was wrong. It only made things worse. I was a fool to think that any man, or god for that matter, was above the temptation that came with a power such as this. I have since learned the error of my ways and will make amends for it by taking the trident someplace where it can harm humanity no more." The Magician made his way toward the exit.

"Wait a minute, so that's just it? *I'm sorry my invention fucked up your lives and killed everybody you care about*, and you think that will suffice?" DeMona asked heatedly.

"Hardly, DeMona. No amount of apologies can make up for what has happened to all of you and the things you lost, but I have no control over what has happened, only what will become," the Magician told her. "I regret the things and people you have lost, but without those losses, you would not have been brought together and would not be prepared for the battle to come."

"What battle? What are you talking about, old man?" DeMona asked.

"You will understand in time. Just know that this isn't the last time you lot will find yourselves called into the service of the light."

"Wait, what about Gabriel's soul? He sacrificed himself to save us," she said.

"No need to fret over the boy. I will keep his spirit and the Nimrod safe and out of the reach of humans. Until we meet again, for the *real* battle, fare thee well, champions." The Magician smiled and vanished with the Nimrod.

"Okay, am I the only one who is more confused now than I was before he showed up?" Asha asked.

"No, you're not the only one," Gilgamesh said.

"And what did he mean by *real* battle?" Morgan asked.

"I guess we'll find out soon enough. Let's just make sure we're ready when it comes," Rogue said.

EPILOGUE

Gilgamesh chartered a private plane to fly them all back to New York City, and Jackson picked them up from the airport. He had a million questions about what had happened, but nobody had the strength to recount the story at the moment. They were tired, beat up, and thankful to be alive. They had survived the battle at Raven Wood, but it only raised more questions. The battle between the dark forces and the new champions had ended, but the war was just beginning.

Lydia and Finnious decided to stay with Jonas at the scrap yard. Together with Jackson and Morgan, they would try to pick up the pieces of Sanctuary and rebuild a newer and better great house. With Jonas's blessing, they would use the scrap yard as their foundation. When they were done, they would open their doors to any and all supernatural creatures who needed a safe haven, or protection from the things that went bump in the night. Cristobel and Mavis declined Gilgamesh's invitation to return them to Midland and the Iron Mountains, opting to instead help their people by aiding in the efforts to rebuild Sanctuary. They were a ragtag bunch, but they were family nonetheless.

Rogue would go back to his life of private investigator by day and pain in the ass to law-breaking supernaturals by night. He offered to give DeMona and Asha jobs, but they had other plans. DeMona wanted to travel, seeking out others of her kind who, like her mother, had grown tired of the war and wanted to do something different with their lives.

Asha and the new Lucy became inseparable, like sisters. She made it her life's mission to teach the child the ways of the coven and make sure she grew up to be an upstanding witch, but it was hard to do so with her still being a wanted criminal by the courts of witches and warlocks. For as long as Dutch was out there somewhere, spewing lies, she and Lucy would never have a fair shot. She would be forever hunted until she cleared her name, which is what she set out to do once her strength returned.

The White Queen, Angelique, was surprised when Asha showed up on her doorstep one day, demanding a fair trial for the crimes she had been accused of committing. Dutch tried to petition to have Asha turned over to him immediately, but the White Queen wouldn't hear of it. They had been searching for her for quite some time to put her to death, so for her to march willingly into the White Court made Angelique curious to hear what she had to say.

Asha could feel the accusing eyes on her as she strolled through the great hall, holding Lucy by the hand. The little girl was frightened, but Asha assured her that everything would be okay. Emissaries from all four courts, Black, White, Red, and Green, were in attendance, waiting to hear the fate of the witch who had been accused of betraying them all to the dark order. Sitting on an elevated chair, draped in her signature white fur, was Angelique. Standing next to her was Dutch. He looked nervous, and that made Asha smile.

"Greetings, Queen of the White Court. I thank you for accepting my invitation—" Asha began.

"Spare me the bullshit, Asha. You are either very brave or very foolish to come here with the charges levied against you. You stand accused of murdering one of my most cherished pupils, as well as betraying the Black Court. What say you?" Angelique asked.

Asha shrugged. "A little of both, I guess. Look, we can skip all the bull and get right to it. My name has been dragged through the mud, and I'm here to clean it up."

"And how do you plan to do that?" Dutch asked.

"By proving that you're a lying piece of shit," Asha snapped at him.

"Little bitch, I'll kill you." Dutch took a step toward Asha, but Angelique's guards cut him off.

"You'll do nothing but be silent. If there will be blood spilled in my house, it will be spilled by me, do you understand?" Angelique turned her cold blue eyes from Dutch to Asha and back again. "Now, the courier you sent said you have proof to back your claim. Where is this proof?"

"Right here." Asha nudged the little girl forward. Lucy looked around nervously at the other witches and warlocks. "This child is the person I stand accused of murdering, but as you can see, she is very much alive."

Angelique's eyes narrowed. "Do you take me for blind? Lucy Brisbane is who you are accused of murdering, not this child."

"This child *is* Lucy." Asha gave her the short version of what had happened. "I know it's a fantastic story, Queen, but you of all people have spent the most time around Lucy, so who better to verify the magical aura of this child to prove what I have said today?"

Angelique stared at the child for a long while, poking and prodding her with her magic. After her investigation, she covered her mouth in shock. "By the Goddess!"

"Exactly, Your Highness. As you can see, this is indeed Lucy Brisbane, at least her spirit," Asha said.

"Even if your story about the body swap is true, what of the other charges? What of your betrayal of your court? How will you prove that?" Dutch challenged.

"With this." Asha tossed a small parcel at Angelique's feet.

Dutch looked at it suspiciously. "Careful, my queen, it could be contaminated with blood magic."

"Good point, which is why I'm going to let you do the honors of opening it," Angelique told him.

Dutch didn't like it, but he did it. Carefully he unwrapped the package and produced a sapphire ring. When he saw it, his bowels almost gave out.

Angelique dropped down from her chair and snatched it from Dutch. She moved amazingly quick, and before anyone could tell what was happening, she had a dagger at Asha's throat. "You dare insult me by throwing the ring of my murdered brother at my feet?"

"Not an insult, Angelique, but proof. Proof that you've got a bigger rat in your kitchen than little old me," Asha said. "This ring was stolen from the man who murdered your brother, the White King. That man." Asha jabbed her finger at Dutch accusingly.

Dutch laughed weakly. "She's lying; she could've gotten that ring from anywhere."

"True, but I didn't get it from anywhere. I got it from your hiding place at the club, where you vainly kept it hidden for years, instead of getting rid of it. Tell me, King, what fool of a killer keeps the smoking gun?" Asha asked, drawing a laugh from those in attendance.

"I'll cut your tongue out for the lies you have told here today," Dutch threatened.

"If they are lies, there is a simple ritual which will prove it. I'm willing to sit here and wait until the White Queen traces the origins of this ring back to the White King's killer, are you?" Asha challenged.

Dutch looked around at the two dozen sets of eyes on him. He felt like he was on trial instead of Asha. He looked down at the ring pinched between Angelique's fingers and cursed himself for being so vain that he insisted on keeping it as a trophy instead of destroying it and his secret with it.

"Death to all of you!" Dutch raised his hands to cast a spell and was immediately tackled by Angelique's personal guard.

"Take him below and wait for me. I am going to see to my brother's murderer personally."

"Unhand me, I am the Black King. You risk civil war if you harm me!" Dutch threatened as they dragged him, kicking and screaming, down to Angelique's torture chamber. Asha had envied Dutch all of her life, but not at that moment. Angelique's love of torture was legendary among all of the courts. For killing her brother, there was no way she was going to let Dutch die swiftly.

"It seems I owe you an apology," Angelique said.

"You don't owe me anything. I just want my name cleared," Asha replied.

Angelique nodded. "Done." She looked to Lucy. "And what should we do about this one?"

"We've just been kind of winging it so far," Asha admitted.

"Well, I made a promise to her mother and I intend to keep it." Angelique knelt down so that she was eye level with Lucy. "Would you like to stay with me at my mansion and learn magic from me?"

"I would love to learn magic from you, Ms. Queen, but if it's okay, I'd like to stay with my big sister Asha. It doesn't look like you old guys have much fun around here."

Both Asha and Angelique looked at each other dumbfounded. "Well, one thing is for sure, she's as opinionated as the old Lucy." Angelique laughed. "Fair enough, you can stay with Asha if it's okay with her."

"Is it?" Lucy looked up at Asha with pleading eyes.

"Of course it is." Asha smiled.

"Then that's settled, the child will stay with you, Asha, but these doors are always open. That invitation is for both of you. Oh and before I forget." Angelique summoned one of her attendants. The girl came forward holding a small cage containing a ferret. "What would a witch be without her familiar?" She handed the cage to Lucy.

"Can I keep it?" Lucy asked excitedly.

"Yes, but it was never mine to give."

Lucy stuck her finger in the cage, and the connection between her and ferret was instant. "I think I'll call him Tikki."

"That sounds like a fine name to me. Now, on to more pressing business." Angelique turned to Asha. "In light of what has happened, the Black Court is without a leader. The position is yours if you want it. I think you've earned it."

Asha thought about it. Since she was a little girl, she had lived to be Mistress of the Hunt, but here Angelique was offering to turn the entire Black Court over to her. It was a very tempting offer. "If it's all the same to you, I'll pass on that, Angelique."

Her refusal caused a stir in the crowd.

"Asha, maybe you want to think about it before refusing. If you sit on the Black Throne, no one will ever be able to question whether you belong or not again. You'll be among family."

"You know, all I ever wanted was to be accepted by other witches, but what I've learned is that I don't need approval from others to belong. Family isn't about politics, it's about love and I've got all the love I need right here." She hugged Lucy to her. "Now, if you'll excuse us, we've got a movie to catch." Asha and Lucy headed for the door.

"Asha." Angelique stopped her. "Take care of her. She's a special child."

Asha nodded. "Nobody knows that better than I do. Come on, kid." Asha took her by the hand. She and Lucy strolled out of Angelique's mansion and into the afternoon sun to see what adventures the day held for them.

It was almost the next morning when Rogue finally made it back to his apartment. His adventures with Gabriel and the others had him spent, and all he wanted to do was sleep. His body and mind were dog tired.

When he slipped his key into his apartment door, an uneasy feeling crept over him. He shrugged off his fatigue and focused on what was wrong. One of the wards on his apartment had been broken. It was done with such subtlety that

Rogue probably wouldn't have noticed if his body wasn't still so overly sensitive to magic after escaping the Devil's Trap. He drew both of his revolvers and entered his apartment.

Rogue's shadow eyes scanned the darkened apartment, searching for signs of danger. All was as it had been when he left. He was beginning to think that maybe his cat, Mr. Jynx, had accidentally tripped the ward when it hit him that he hadn't seen the cat since he entered the apartment. Normally Mr. Jynx pounced on him as soon as he crossed the threshold, but there was no sign of him.

Tapping into his magic, Rogue sent a signal through the shadows that was akin to an electric shock. There was a yelp, and someone jumped out of the corner. Rogue didn't even think about it when he sent a wave of shadow rolling across the room, pinning the intruder to the wall. Rogue was angry; after all he'd been through, he was in no mood for more bullshit. Whoever had been foolish enough to break into his home would regret it.

"You picked the wrong house on the right night, buddy." Rogue moved toward the intruder, tightening the shadows as he walked, choking the life out of whomever it was. When Rogue got closer, he focused on the intruder's face, as that was the only part of his body that was still visible. The rest of him was consumed by shadows. When he made out the intruder's features in the moonlight, he gasped and abruptly released him from the shadows.

Rogue clapped his hands and the track lights came on. "Are you out of your mind? I could've killed you!"

The intruder slowly got up off the floor, coughing and wheezing from almost having his chest crushed. "Bullshit, you never did have the stomach for blood."

"A lot has changed since the last time we saw each other," Rogue told him, using the shadows to give him a soft push into the chair under the lamp.

"Apparently so." The intruder gave a raspy laugh. In the pale yellow light, his face was more visible. His dark skin was worn and leathery. Stringy gray dreads hung down from the sides of his balding head. He was elderly, but his body still held some of its youthful definition.

"State your business, and get the fuck out of my house, Jacob!" Rogue demanded.

When Jacob looked up at Rogue, his eyes were milky as if his vision were failing him, and he squinted to focus. "What's the matter, John? Ain't you happy to see your baby brother?"